THE
OF THE
YEAR

Enjoy the story...
Bonnie Howell

BONNIE HOWELL

eLectio Publishing
Little Elm, TX
www.eLectioPublishing.com

The Story of the Year
By Bonnie Howell

Copyright 2017 by Bonnie Howell. All rights reserved.
Cover Design by eLectio Publishing.

ISBN-13: 978-1-63213-242-0

Published by eLectio Publishing, LLC
Little Elm, Texas
http://www.eLectioPublishing.com

Printed in the United States of America

5 4 3 2 1 eLP 21 20 19 18 17

The eLectio Publishing creative team is comprised of: Kaitlyn Campbell, Emily Certain, Lori Draft, Court Dudek, Jim Eccles, Sheldon James, and Christine LePorte.

Without limiting the rights under copyright reserved above, no part of this publication may be reproduced, stored in or introduced into a retrieval system, or transmitted, in any form, or by any means (electronic, mechanical, photocopying, recording, or otherwise), without the prior written permission of both the copyright owner and the above publisher of this book.

If you purchased this book without a cover, you should be aware that this book is stolen property. It was reported as "unsold and destroyed" to the publisher and neither the author nor the publisher has received any payment for the "stripped book."

The scanning, uploading, and distribution of this book via the Internet or via any other means without the permission of the publisher is illegal and punishable by law. Please purchase only authorized electronic editions, and do not participate in or encourage electronic piracy of copyrighted materials. Your support of the author's rights is appreciated.

Publisher's Note

The publisher does not have any control over and does not assume any responsibility for author or third-party websites or their content.

This is a work of fiction. Names, characters, places, and incidents either are the product of the author's imagination or are used fictitiously, and any resemblance to actual persons, living or dead, business establishments, events, or locales is entirely coincidental.

THE STORY OF THE YEAR

ONE

The roar of the flames filled the night, lighting up the darkness with a strange and foreboding orange hue, accentuated by the blinding white bolts of lightning still shattering the sky just to the west, and drowning out the crash of the thunder with their own ominous wind. The thick, acrid smoke choked her as KC raced down the worn steps of the wooden fire lookout tower, just as the fire began to lick at the legs of the old structure. Her feet slipped on the precarious shale covered path, but she managed to keep them under her in her race down the rocky slope. She prayed silently and continually all the way.

God, help me! Jesus, give me strength!

The long, unstable, mile-long hike down usually took about twenty cautious minutes, but she negotiated it at breakneck speed in record time. The sound grew even louder as the structure caught fire above her, lighting up like a torch, spewing ashes and debris down toward her. Barely able to catch her breath, KC reached the gravel road below and did not slow down as she continued her race down the mountain, the fire above her growling at her escape, rushing after her in its vicious attempt to catch and consume her. The adrenalin rush that fueled her speed was giving way to exhaustion as she ran on, one foot in front of the other.

Just as she felt that the fire had won and she could not run another step, bright headlights pierced the dense, smoke-filled night ahead of her. A pickup truck screeched to a halt just feet in front of her, and the driver jumped out and ran toward her, reaching her just as her exhausted legs gave out.

"Nick! I knew you would come!"

Putting his arm around her, he led her to the safety of the front passenger seat and then ran around to jump in behind the wheel.

"Hold on!"

THE STORY OF THE YEAR

Nick spun the truck around and began anew the race down the mountain. The orange monster behind them was reflected in the rear-view mirror, and KC sat transfixed at the sight, barely able to breathe. As they sped around the corner, a bolt of lightning split a tall tree, sending it crashing across the road just fifty feet in front of them. The tires of the speeding truck slid on the loose gravel as Nick slammed on the brakes, sending them careening toward the ditch on the side of the road.

"Lord, we need your help right now!" Nick called out loudly.

TWO

Strange sounds and urgent voices mingled with the strong smell of smoke and the bright flashing lights in the recesses of KC's memory.

So tired. More sleep. What is that annoying beeping?

KC opened her eyes to the morning light streaming in the window across the unfamiliar room. Wires and tubes connected to her arms and hands on each side impeded her ability to move more than a little bit, the effort causing pain in her head and pretty much every other spot in her entire body. A hospital monitoring machine beside her beeped on steadily, which she figured was a good sign, as her foggy brain cleared and she remembered the hectic rush down the mountain with the fire close behind her.

The fire!

She managed to pull herself up a little higher on the pillow. There was Nick, slumped in a chair by the side of her bed, his chest rising and falling rhythmically in sleep, his arm in a sling. His hair fell endearingly over his forehead, and she reached out impulsively to touch him.

She must have whimpered a bit at the movement, because Nick suddenly jarred awake and reached out his good hand toward her.

"KC! You're awake!" The relief was evident in his voice. "Thank you, Lord!"

Nick stood up, his own pain showing on his face.

"Is it broken? Your arm?"

"Yeah, it is. My arm and your head. How are you feeling?"

"I'm alive, which is a miracle in itself. I remember us driving down the mountain and the tree falling in front of us and not much after that."

Nick stroked her cheek gently as he brushed a soft wave of her hair back. He loved the color of her hair, like dark winter wheat. She hated it, not blonde, not brunette. She looked fragile and diminutive under the blankets, her tall frame eclipsed by the machines surrounding her. Nick bent down, as if he meant to kiss her, but he hovered just above her, looking into her brown eyes with concern in his own.

"God was watching over us, that's for sure. My team arrived just moments after the crash. We are both going to be just fine."

Just then, a doctor swished into the room, followed by a nurse who shooed Nick out and attended to all of the wires and tubes and other duties. Then a sweet older woman dressed in pink brought her some pudding and tea, and she fell back into a drowsy sleep.

KC slept on and off the rest of the morning, waking to eat when the surprisingly palatable lunch arrived, and getting up briefly with the help of a nurse. She woke later that afternoon to find her parents standing at the foot of her bed.

"Don't you ever do anything like that again!" her mother chided, "you scared ten years off our lives! Ken, tell her not to do anything dangerous again!"

"Hush, Mary! I cannot wait to read all about it in your newspaper article, KC."

KC grinned widely, even though the effort hurt her head, at the familiar bantering between her parents. If she did not change the subject, they could go back and forth for hours.

"Please tell me you are here to take me home."

The door opened on cue and the doctor came in, giving her instructions to rest and not exert herself and officially releasing her. Dad left the room to move the car, and Mom helped her into the clean clothes that she had brought from her closet at home. The ones she was wearing when she arrived at the hospital were trashed. KC buttoned up her sweater, looking at the door yet again.

Where is Nick?

She needed to see him so badly it hurt more than her tender head.

The door opened and she looked up hopefully. Dad came in, grinning at her disappointed look.

"What's the matter? Not happy to see old Dad?" He moved aside and Nick came into the room, and KC felt as if she could at last breathe again.

He came close to her and reached out, gently moving her bangs aside to see the impressive bruise covering her forehead. If her parents had not been in the room, she would have hugged him.

"Let's go!" Dad interrupted the moment and brought her back to reality. She was loaded into a wheelchair, and pushed out of the door and down the hall so fast her head literally was spinning. KC called out frantically.

"Nick!"

Mom reached for her hand as she walked beside her. "Relax, he is coming, too."

KC looked confused.

Mom spoke in her reassuring, calm voice. "We could not leave Nick to fend for himself with only one good arm, could we? Especially when he saved your life!"

Nick caught up to her and walked on her other side. Along the way, he picked up the small bag that he had left in a chair at the nurse's station.

They made a quick stop at KC's apartment, where her mother ran up the stairs to pick up some clothes and personal items. KC sat contentedly next to Nick in the back seat as they wove their way through the Portland city traffic and out onto the highway leading toward the small town of Pineville, Oregon and her childhood home.

Nick dozed off, likely the effect of the pain medicine they had given him for his broken arm. KC was happy just to sit next to him.

Has it only been a little over three weeks since we first met?

She could not help smiling as she remembered.

"KC Adams?" Nick stretched out his hand for a formal handshake, his forced smile as stiff as his manner. She would have found him attractive in other circumstances, but the look in his eyes conveyed impatience, not interest. A firefighter for the Department of Forestry, he was all business. "I'm Nick Evans. I'll be taking you to the Iliana Lookout Tower. You are not taking all of *this*?" His look said it all.

Glancing down, KC surveyed her sleeping bag, backpack with her tablet and writing essentials, rolling suitcase with her clothes and shoes, makeup case, and box of canned food and snacks.

What's the problem?

"We have to hike up a steep, slippery mountain path nearly a mile long and carry everything on our backs. Unless you have a donkey in that bag, you can take the backpack and sleeping bag. Put what you can in the backpack. I'll be bringing your food supplies and water."

Her face red from embarrassment and indignation, KC huffed back to the parking lot and stowed everything she did not absolutely need in the trunk of her old car, stuffing what clothes she could fit and her favorite tea from her snack box into her backpack.

The nerve of that guy!

Nick softened his attitude on the long drive up the mountain, as he began to share his knowledge and love of the area. His stoic expression changed when he talked about the old lookout tower, which was scheduled to be replaced the next year with automated equipment.

"Iliana was built in 1938. The old wooden tower has overseen the mountain and the forest she protects faithfully for a long, long time. I remember making the hike up when I was just a young boy. It made a lasting impression on me. Did you know that she doubled as a lookout for enemy airplanes during WWII?"

"She?"

"Sure, *Iliana*. And just wait until you see her long legs!"

Men!

"Several famous writers have been summer fire lookouts here, too. I know that you are really going to enjoy your time here."

KC smiled when he mentioned the writers. After all, writing was what had brought her to this volunteer position in the first place.

"I am only planning to be the fire lookout for a month, as an assignment from my editor at the newspaper. I write 'Around the Block'. Have you read my column? No? Well, I mostly write about local events and human interest stories."

"Not sports?"

"Definitely *not* sports."

The conversation between them flowed easily. She did not want to like Nick, but she couldn't help it. Tall, broad shouldered, with dark brown hair unfairly thick and wavy, incredibly blue eyes, this was a man most women would fall for.

Not me, of course.

KC smiled at the memory and laid her head on Nick's shoulder, falling asleep to the rhythm of the moving car, the soft music playing on the radio, and the warmth of Nick's presence next to her.

THREE

Snuggled comfortably on the old leather couch in the family room, under her favorite red chenille throw, with Nick similarly tucked into the large recliner, KC gave a contented sigh. She knew that the pampering Mom had insisted on would soon grow old, but for now it was nice to just rest her painful head and sore body.

"Mmm. This is nice."

Dad poked his head around the door to check on them yet again. "Do you need anything, KC? You OK, Nick?"

"We're doing just great, Ken!"

The table next to the recliner was piled high with snacks of all kinds in easy reach of his good arm, his water glass and tea cup recently refilled. Nick kicked his foot out from under the blanket covering him and stretched his toes toward the sofa, tapping KC gently on the leg. He barely missed hitting the coffee table in front of her that had an equal number of readily available snacks and drinks.

"Hey, is it always like this when you come home? I might just suggest that your folks adopt me!" Nick grinned as he always did when joking about being adopted.

Over the course of the past three weeks, they had grown as close as old friends, talking in the confines of the little lookout building on the quiet mountaintop. It still amazed KC how quickly they had clicked, how easily they could talk to each other, how comfortable they were together. She had never made a friend so easily. Nick managed to visit often, bringing water or supplies, picking up the flash drive that contained her latest column to send to the newspaper, or just checking on her in his time off.

Nick told her that he had been orphaned at the tender age of ten and grew up in a series of foster homes. KC was an only child, but had a big extended family, the kind of family Nick said he had always dreamed of having.

"The Hampton family took me in just before my last year of high school, when I had come very close to dropping out. They were a strong Christian couple in their late sixties, and they showed me real love. Betty Hampton used to say 'Nick, God loves you and I love you. Nothing you do or say will ever change that.' That kind of love changed my life. I stopped being the rebel, and focused on school and sports.

"George and Betty took me to church with them, and I came to believe in the God who loves me, forgives me, and calls me His child. You can't know what that is like for a kid who lived most of his life as nobody's child."

"Do you still keep in touch with the Hamptons?"

"No, my foster parents died in a car accident during my first year of college. But I know that I will one day see them again."

KC told him that she was also a Christian. He never knew what she was actually thinking.

I wish I had that much faith.

As Nick dozed off again, whether from the pain medicine or an overdose of snacks, KC laid back against the pillows and thought about her own faith. She had believed in God since she was a young child, and walked down to the front of the church to accept Jesus publicly as her Savior. Secure in the love of her family, safe in her small town, that faith had never been tested.

I was so naïve.

***

Leaving home for the first time to attend the University of Arizona's School of Journalism, KC found herself thrown into a noisy, chaotic, and often faithless world. This world was as different as night and day from her life in the small town in Oregon. Focused on her studies, she avoided the parties and drinking and other activities often associated with life at a university. She had not even dated until her last year when she had met Derrick.

True love.

He was good-looking and smart, a talented athlete, and she was the envy of all of the girls in her dorm. They walked down the aisle at their graduation ceremony hand-in-hand. KC silently envisioned a different walk down another aisle with Derrick, not too far in her future. Immediately after graduation, he enlisted in the Air Force as an officer, his goal to be a pilot. She returned home to Pineville to work for her parents in their hardware store and to look for her dream journalism job. No dream was too big. She applied in London and New York and wherever her Internet job searches took her. She was unwavering and persistent, accepting each rejection without losing her hope. She was sure that the perfect job was just around the corner, if she just persevered in applying. The letter came from Derrick's mother just a few weeks later. He had been killed in a training accident. She failed miserably in this first true test of her faith. She blamed God.

How could You let this happen?

The next few years living at home were boring but safe. She worked at the hardware store for Dad, and wrote for the local newspaper. It was really more like a newsletter, paid with a free subscription, but at least she was writing. She attended church as expected, but her heart was not in it. She stayed in her safe little bedroom where she had been raised, and let her mind and her heart remain numb.

And then there was Geoffrey. An old high school boyfriend, he returned to Pineville to set up his veterinary practice just has he had always planned.

"Come to lunch with me."

"I'm very busy."

"Would you like to go to a movie?"

"No, thank you."

There was no spark between them. Still, he kept trying. "How about ...?"

Not interested. Not after Derrick. Not ever.

THE STORY OF THE YEAR

***

The doorbell rang, breaking the silence of the afternoon, waking Nick. He stretched and smiled at her, and KC forgot the pain of her past in the contentment of her present.

"Kerry, dear, look who is here to see you!" Geoffrey was ushered into the room. "Geoffrey, have a seat. Would you like some tea?"

Really, Mom? What part of not interested don't you understand?

After an awkward introduction, Nick threw off his covers and stood up, reaching out his good arm for a polite but firm handshake.

"Uh, these are for you." Geoffrey thrust a large, unwieldy bouquet of flowers toward KC. She managed to untangle herself from the throw and pillows and stood up, sitting down quickly as brief dizziness overtook her. Immediately, Geoffrey rushed to one side and Nick to the other to assist her. Mom reached for the flowers and took them to the kitchen to put them in a vase, totally oblivious to the tension in the room.

"I'm fine! Will you both just sit down!"

Nick returned to the recliner, wincing as he sat down, having reached out instinctively with his broken arm to help KC. Geoffrey sat on the edge of the small flowered chair her mother preferred, looking fairly uncomfortable.

Just then, Dad came into the room and sat next to KC on the cluttered couch, taking her hand in his. "What do you think of my girl here Geoff? Have you read her latest columns?"

KC stifled a giggle. No one called Geoffrey anything but Geoffrey.

Good one, Dad!

Geoffrey appeared unfazed, however, as he pulled a manila envelope from his inside jacket pocket and removed a stack of newspaper clippings.

"I have been reading every column you wrote for 'Around the Block'. See? I have clipped out each column, and I plan to put them in a scrapbook soon. Fascinating!"

KC grimaced. That was not a word she would have used. Boring. Mundane. Uninspired. But never fascinating. She was so excited to get a real job at a real newspaper; she packed up and moved to Portland immediately. It was time to get on with her own career, her own life. Her assigned column, 'Around the Block', fell somewhere between the famed 'Around the World' column and the obituaries, being closer to the latter than the former.

KC's columns included an exciting piece about the upcoming book club fundraiser, and the egg hunt at the county courthouse. She documented the cutting of the ribbon at a new supermarket, and she covered the remodeling of a landmark apartment building. She had also found thrilling stories in the human-interest category, such as the retirement of the local animal control officer, and the reunion of ninety-year-old twins, separated at birth and raised in different homes. Nothing in her articles was earth shattering or Pulitzer Prize worthy. Lately, she had been writing a lot of columns on cats. Six weeks ago, it was 'Widow's Fortune Left to her Cat FooFoo' and a month ago, her byline was on a story with the headline 'Twenty Pound Tabby Named Fluffy Foils Cat Burglar'.

Not the journalistic excellence I dreamed about when I graduated, but it's a start.

She wondered what the literary snobs she studied journalism with would think of her now. She saw on social media that the class valedictorian had a novel on the bestseller list.

Overachiever!

Geoffrey seemed oblivious to the fact that her mind had wandered off.

"Cats are very intelligent animals, much smarter than dogs, in my estimation. Why I once knew a cat . . ."

Mom came back into the room and sat down on the other end of the couch, effectively sandwiching KC in and giving her no avenue for escape. At that moment, Nick moaned and rubbed the shoulder above his broken arm.

THE STORY OF THE YEAR

"Mary, is it time for my pain medication, yet? My arm is killing me!"

"Oh dear, of course! I will get it right now."

Jumping up immediately, Mom went into the kitchen to get the prescription bottle, and Dad quickly seized the moment to usher a confused Geoffrey out of the front door.

"Thanks for coming by, Geoff, but these two need their rest. It might be a good idea to give them a week or so before visiting again." They could barely hear Geoffrey's muttered response as the door closed.

KC flashed Nick a look of gratitude, and stretched back out on the couch with a little grin. When Mom returned, both Nick and KC appeared to be sleeping, so she set the prescription bottle on the table and left them quietly alone. Nick's snoring followed a few moments later.

KC readjusted her pillow and tucked the throw more closely around her legs, but she could not sleep. How comfortable she was with Nick, as if they had been friends for years rather than months.

It's too bad that he works at such a dangerous job. There is no way I would take a chance on love with someone who flirts with death every time he goes out. Besides, we are just friends.

KC smiled to herself, and dozed off.

FOUR

KC groaned. "No more toast! We are both going to be too fat to get up off the couch if you keep this up. It was a wonderful breakfast, thanks Mom!"

Nick pulled up his shirt and looked at his belly and added, "I think it is too late" which earned him a playful slap on his good shoulder.

Leaving the table clean up to her insistent mother, KC started back toward the family room. Nick grabbed her hand and led her toward the front door instead. "We need fresh air. No more couch sitting for us this morning! This is a beautiful day, isn't it?"

It had been three days since she came home from the hospital, and KC was doing much better. Nick stopped taking any pain medicine after the second morning, and was trying his best not to take his broken arm out of the sling and move it around. He was not used to being inactive.

"Wait right here."

With KC comfortably settled in on the porch swing, Nick went back inside and returned with copies of the newspapers that her parents had saved for her during her time up the mountain. "Read! I want to hear all of your thoughts on your adventure in the lookout."

Smiling, KC took the newspapers and sorted them in the order they were written.

***

Around the Block

June 17

This reporter will be deviating from my usual coverage of local activities to report to you my amazing summer adventure in the mountains southeast of Portland. I have taken the opportunity to fill in for a month as a firewatcher

THE STORY OF THE YEAR

at the Iliana Lookout Tower. Come along with me on this escapade, as you read about life at Iliana.

My first day was a mixture of excitement and anticipation. Once free of the baggage which I admittedly had overpacked, I made the drive up into the mountains in the company of a professional firefighter, well versed in the history of the old tower. Built in the late 1930s, the wooden tower has watched over the surrounding area for generations. It is scheduled to be replaced with the latest technology such as computers with smoke-detecting pattern-recognition software, GPS, Internet, cell access, and automated digital cameras, early next year. The building itself is slated to be dismantled and reassembled near a local museum, never to serve its purpose again. Such is the fate of many of these old towers, which mark the end of an era for the loyal lookouts who have manned them over the decades.

The walk to the tower itself was up a mile of slippery, shale-covered trail with steep switchbacks and amazing views. Nothing, however, compared to the view once we reached the top, where I was surrounded by 360 degrees of beautiful.

I settled in after a thorough training in how to use the equipment, including a fire finder that measures the distance from and the direction of a fire, a two-way radio, and a good pair of binoculars. Alone and at peace, I made myself a cup of my favorite tea and stood out on the catwalk, watching the light of the sun touch the edge of the trees as it headed toward the distant horizon. The darkness came quickly on that moonless night, and the stars appeared one by one until the sky was as bright as I had ever seen. I am going to love this assignment, especially sharing it with you.

Until Next week,

KC Adams

***

"That was beautifully written, KC. You have a real talent with words!" Nick reached across with his good arm and squeezed her hand. "Go on, read the next one."

Blushing slightly at his praise, KC opened the newspaper from the following week.

***

Around the Block

June 24

I have been in the Iliana Lookout Tower for a week now, and I have found my rhythm. I am pleased to say that I have become adept at using the equipment. I memorized the forest and mountains that surround me so that if someone builds a campfire miles away, I can detect and identify the smoke. I am learning to make do with the food provided, though I admit to wishing that they delivered pizza up here now and then. The firefighter who brought me up here has been nice enough to bring me additional supplies and to check on my progress.

I can see why so many famous writers have become lookouts. A quiet life, this job affords the opportunity to tune in to your deepest creative thoughts without the noise of music or phones or television or other people talking. If you have never seen the sun come up over a distant mountain as you stood huddled in a warm blanket, holding a hot cup of tea in your hand and seeing the mist of your breath visible in the cold dawn air, or listened to the sound of the birds as they flew overhead on their way to a familiar and compulsory place, or lay down alone in the dark of the night with no outside light or a single sound to mar a perfect sleep, then you need to come to the mountain. It will renew your soul.

A month will not be long enough to fully appreciate this life. Today I made my way down the mountain a short

THE STORY OF THE YEAR

distance to a little meadow where comfrey flowers were blooming. I picked some of the flowers to brighten up my new home, and took some of the leaves to make an herbal tea. A little squirrel chatted with me briefly, before making his way back to the safety of the trees. He and I are going to be good friends.

Tonight, the clouds are darkening, and a thunderstorm is predicted. I am in close contact with the dispatcher on the radio. Whoa! The lightning is quite far away but extremely bright against the dark clouds, and the thunder is louder than I have ever heard. I admit to being on edge, figuratively and literally, as I sit on the little wooden stool provided, just to be sure that I am safe, even though the lookout tower has an ample lightning rod. Here comes the rain. If I thought that the distant thunder was loud, the pounding of the rain on the metal roof is even louder. I will have a long and busy night. I just saw two more distant flashes of lightning, and realized that being on my tablet as I write this column is probably not very wise.

Until next week,

KC Adams

***

"Really? Writing your column during a thunderstorm?"

Just as she was about to read the third column, a big, black car drove up and parked out front, along the curb. Curious, KC shielded her eyes from the bright sun and watched as the editor-in-chief of her newspaper came out from the passenger seat. Turning toward her with a big smile on his face, he made his way up the walk.

"KC, so good to see you up! How are you feeling after your frightening experience with the fire, not to mention the accident?"

"Much better, thank you, Mr. Knitzer." KC was stunned at the unexpected appearance of the editor. She had only seen him briefly in a few meetings and once on a long and very uncomfortable elevator ride to the top floor of her office building to retrieve a file. He had never actually spoken to her before. And yet here he was, standing on her steps.

"Won't you come in?" KC stood up awkwardly from the moving swing.

"Sit, sit, my dear. I only have a moment. I just wanted to check on you. And is this the fireman who saved your life?"

KC introduced Nick, who was standing next to the swing.

"Well, well. Nice to meet you. Very nice indeed."

Nick stepped out from beside the swing and reached out to shake his hand, and was rewarded with a damp but firm handshake in response.

"You too."

"I do hope we will have your column in time for printing in three days. This series has been very popular, very popular. And after the news of the big fire, our readership is anxious to hear from you about it. As are we all, of course." He handed her a plastic shoebox, which she could see with a glance was stuffed full of get-well cards and letters. "These came to the office, but you should also check your email and your newspaper social media pages. The response has been incredible. Incredible."

Nick began to speak up, but KC interrupted him and answered, "I will get on it right away. I will send it in no later than three tomorrow afternoon."

"Good, good. Well, you two take care now." With that, he turned on his heel and scurried down the sidewalk to climb back into the car, which drove off down the road as quickly as it had come.

"Don't say it!" KC held up her hand to stop Nick from making any comments. "I am doing just fine. I can write this column."

She started to stand up, but Nick sat down beside her and reached for her hand. "Can we just sit for a few more minutes and read the last column before you go in?"

THE STORY OF THE YEAR

"Sure. A few more minutes won't matter."

Smiling, KC set the box aside and shuffled through the newspapers, pulling out the last column that she had written just a few days before the fire, pleased that Nick was interested.

***

Around the Block

July 1

The storm last week was both beautiful and frightening, raw power unleashed on the world around me with no distractions to cause me to tune it out. While I sat on the little wooden stool, watching carefully for any fires that might have started as a result of the lightning, the rain began to let up in its intensity. As the storm moved off toward the east, an amazing sense of peace came over me. Happily, there were no fires and I was able to get some sleep, awakened with the bright sun shining on my face, heralding a fresh, new day.

I stood outside that morning, vowing to never take the tranquility and beauty around me for granted. It was just one unfortunate lightning strike away from oblivion. My little squirrel friend came for a brief visit, but the rest of the day was quiet.

A few evenings later, as I sat reading by the light of a battery-operated lantern, the cool breeze from a window offering a respite from the heat of the day, a movement above me caught my attention. I am not afraid of snakes, spiders, bears, or cougars. This was far more menacing! A bat had landed on the beam right over my bed. Now, I don't usually mind sharing, but there was no way that I was going to be able to go to sleep with that bat hanging over my head. After opening all of the doors and windows, I donned my trusty LED headlamp, and armed with a long tree limb that I had been using as a walking staff, I bravely stood by the side of my bed and waved my stick. The bat was too high to even notice. Growing bolder, I climbed onto the little bed built against the wall and hit the beam firmly with the staff. Three things happened. The bat flew around my head once (I am pretty sure I screamed), the board beneath my feet broke, sending me down onto the bed with one leg through to the floor on the bottom, and then the bat flew nonchalantly out of the door.

I extricated myself from the bed and quickly closed all of the windows and the doors in case he changed his mind. I then pulled back my sleeping bag and the thin mattress and surveyed the damage. The main piece of lumber that held up the frame was still attached to the wall. Most of the lattice of wooden cross bars were still solid. But one section of wood had been purposely cut and then just set back in place. I had not broken the bed at all, just displaced this one section.

As I tried to put everything back into place, I noticed something red in the opening under the bed. Laying in an uncomfortable and unnatural position, I managed to reach my arm down through the hole and pulled out an old book. Slightly faded, and layered with years of dust, I had discovered what appears to be a very old diary. Could it be the journal of a lookout from generations ago?

Until next week.

KC Adams

***

KC ended her reading of the last column with a big sigh. "Nick, imagine how close we came to losing that diary in the fire. If I had not given it to you to take back to the office, the contents would always remain a mystery."

"Well, it is safe and sound in a locked drawer in my desk. I never had the opportunity to do any research on who may have written it or when."

"Thank goodness it was spared! I am excited to read it and perhaps find out about the person who wrote it. It can wait until we are both back to work. Speaking of work, I had better get inside and start working on my next column." KC stood up and gave Nick a smile that did not go all the way to her eyes, then went back inside the house.

FIVE

The house was dark and silent with the exception of the desk lamp that illuminated the computer on her father's old desk and the sound of tapping on the keys. Tap, tap, tap ... write one word. Tap, tap, tap ... erase the last two. KC started over again and again, but the words would just not come out right.

"Are you OK?" Nick's question startled her. She had not heard him come out of the guestroom. "How about taking a break for a cup of decaf Earl Gray tea?"

She pushed the chair back without hesitation and followed him into the kitchen where he deftly managed to put on the kettle with one hand while she raided the fridge for some leftovers.

KC glanced at the kitchen clock over the sink. "It's 3:00 a.m. already? No wonder I'm hungry again." She had been trying to write this simple column for so many hours, and promised her editor that she would submit it just twelve hours from now.

What if I just can't do it?

Nick waited patiently at the table while she nibbled on the last of her cake and refilled her tea cup yet again. "Talk to me, KC."

Tears came unbidden. "Every time I try to write about the experience, I re-live the fear of that night. My hands shake and my mouth goes dry and the words will just not come."

Nick just stood up and pulled her to him and held her as she cried, letting go of the fear, letting go of the false bravado that she had shown to all around her since the fire and the accident. He waited patiently in the silence of the early morning, and held her tightly until she stopped crying and pushed back, looking up at him with a smile.

"I guess I needed that."

"Let me tell you about my first fire when I was just eighteen." Nick ushered her back into her father's office and sat down beside her on the little loveseat. "I was the typical, know-it-all teenager,

THE STORY OF THE YEAR

working on a fire crew for the summer as I earned my way through college. I had all of the usual training and the same pack test that they put you through before allowing you to be a lookout."

KC nodded.

"It was late in August and we had a pretty quiet summer up until then. They had us clearing trails and doing some prevention work, when the call came in. A big fire in the steepest terrain around. Started from an unattended campfire, we found out later. Wayne, my crew leader, was getting up there in age, and he had his hands full with a bunch of young guys and gals chomping at the bit to do some real work. We were up on a steep hillside digging hand lines, when the wind shifted, sending the fire our way in a hurry. Hot, flying embers set the trees and brush on fire not far below us, blocking our only route out. Just above us a bulldozer was working the fire line. The operator, Wayne called him a catskinner, drove down to where we were and quickly began clearing brush and debris down to bare earth, creating as much of a firebreak as possible. He started digging as deep a hole as he could through the packed dirt. The air became smokier as the fire grew closer. I remember that I could not take a deep breath. Well, the catskinner drove his bulldozer over the top of the hole, while the rest of us covered each other with water from our pump cans. Wayne called out 'Deploy your fire shelters and climb under the bulldozer!' We were all sweltering hot, and our eyes and throats stung from the smoke, but we made it out alive. That was the most terrifying, unforgettable, frightening moment of my entire life. I was a fairly new Christian, and I prayed through the entire experience as the fire roared around us. *God, please don't let us die!* A plane dropped water over our exit route and eventually stopped the fire in our area in its tracks. We all came out of it OK, but a crew working somewhere below us panicked and tried to run. Four young men did not make it out."

KC squeezed his hand, tears in her eyes. "How were you able to continue doing your job after that?"

"I pretended to be tough, as if it was no big deal. A few days later when I was released from the incident, I went home and cried like a baby. I was not close to the four men who had died, but the fact that it could have been me hit home like a ton of bricks!"

"But you still do that job. You put yourself at risk all the time. I could never do that!"

I could never be with anyone who does that.

"I thought about quitting back then, but there is something about being in the woods and protecting the land that just draws me to it. I determined right there and then to learn all that I could. Now, years later, I strive to be like Wayne, my old crew leader, teaching and protecting those under my care and authority and keeping them from harm. In the winter, when my crew leaves and I am stuck behind a desk doing the paperwork, I miss it. I could never settle for a desk job year-round. But every year, I face the same fear that you did. Fire is a formidable foe and those who are not afraid of it are foolish."

"So, you do understand!"

"Yes, I do." Nick stood up and reached for her hand, pulling her up beside him, then led her to the desk. "I'll just sit over here while you write that column."

***

Around the Block

July 8

The day started out just like any other day in the Iliana Lookout Tower. I checked the weather forecast which called for a 20 percent chance of thunderstorms. I made a cup of tea, and stood out on the catwalk looking out over the mountains and trees under my watch. I had been through a storm just over a week ago; this would be a piece of cake.

I walked down to the meadow later in the afternoon, hoping to see my little squirrel who had neglected to visit me that morning. Not a sign of him. No birds flew in the sky overhead, no insects chirped or buzzed in the grass. Everything was eerily still.

THE STORY OF THE YEAR

I returned to the tower feeling a little more cautious than usual. I checked the distant mountains with my binoculars, but all was quiet. Too quiet.

By late afternoon, huge clouds were building to the west. That evening, the dispatcher on the radio confirmed the impending storm. I closed the windows and latched them as the wind began to pick up. Usually content to walk around the tower in the evenings in my bare feet and flannel pajamas, I stayed in my jeans and T-shirt and put on my running shoes and a hoodie, set my headlamp out on the desk, and prepared for the storm that was coming.

The lightning began far over the western edge of my viewing area. This storm did not bring the rain as the last one had done. The air was hot and dry. I walked outside briefly, but my hair literally stood up on end, and I quickly retreated inside to sit on my stool. The sky grew darker. Then I saw it. The flash was brighter than any I had ever seen before.

The thick column of smoke came soon after I saw the bolt of lightning strike, visible as the sky lit up with successive rounds of sheet lightning. My training kicked in, and I identified the location and distance and called it in. The radio began to have a lot of static as the lightning moved closer to my location, and I finally gave up trying to communicate altogether.

That is when it hit. A lightning bolt that lit up the sky and everything around me. Bright white and crackling, followed just a heartbeat later by a huge roll of thunder. It struck the enormous tree just below the lookout tower, snapping the top as if it was a toothpick, and sending a curtain of flame along the dry grass and brush below. I called the fire in on the radio, but I was not sure I could be heard over the static. The increasing wind whipped the flames to the top of the trees, jumping from tree to tree and moving faster than you can imagine.

The dry grass, brush, and weeds that lead up the slope to the tower caught quickly, and the flames were just touching the legs of the old wooden structure as I decided to leave my post. I began a long and precarious run down the slippery, shale-covered trail toward the road below, the light from my headlamp barely piercing the darkness. I prayed as I ran. I could hear the wooden tower catch fire behind me, the roar of the flames louder than anything I have ever heard. I do not know how I made it down the steep path without falling. Once at the bottom, I kept running down the road, the fire still coming behind me, only slightly slowed as it began its descent down the mountain.

I knew that my strength was failing, and that I could not outrun the flames much longer, when the bright headlights of a pickup truck came into view. The firefighter that has looked out for me over the past three weeks had come to save me. Safely inside the cab of the truck, we turned around and began the drive to safety.

I vaguely remember a flash of lightning and a tree falling across the road. I do not remember the brave fire crew that came to our rescue and kept those flames at bay while they cut the fallen tree out of the way and rushed us to the hospital.

I am happy to report that despite a big bruise on my forehead and a few aches and pains, I am doing well. The Iliana Fire Lookout went out in a dramatic burst of flames, perhaps making a final protest against technology and change. I truly appreciate the cards and emails and comments on my social media pages that you, my loyal readers, have sent to me. The firefighter who saved me (and wishes to remain anonymous) has a broken arm and a very grateful friend for life.

Until next week,

KC Adams

SIX

KC ran a finger over the dust on her bookshelf as she walked by, then set the new backpack down on her bed. The apartment was small, and she could still smell the gasoline from the automotive shop next-door, but at least it was hers and she was home. Her father had dropped Nick off at his office and KC picked up her car, its trunk still containing her overstuffed bags and the snack box that she had packed a month before. Luckily the food was all shelf-stable. The half-dozen boxes of tea went into her cupboard, the canned and packaged food stayed in the box to be given to the local food bank, and the stale cookies went into the trash. A small bag of chocolate, overlooked as she had stuffed things quickly into her backpack, was now a solid mass, and she tossed it quickly before she could give in to the temptation to eat it. She unpacked everything with a smile, remembering the look on Nick's face when he had first met her.

I'm going to miss that look.

On their last morning together at her parent's house, they had hugged, each reluctant to be the first to break the hold. Finally, Nick pulled back and smiled at her.

"I'll be by your apartment first thing on Saturday morning, and I'll bring the red diary with me."

"I am so excited to read it!"

"Yeah, it will give me something to look forward to after a week spent chained to my desk. I just know I will be stuck there the rest of the summer." Though the assignment was understandable with his broken arm, KC knew it was hard for him to embrace. He was used to being active. "From a firefighter to a secretary. Grrr."

KC gently patted his shoulder. "Sorry."

He assured her. "It's a small price to pay for getting you off the burning mountain."

She would miss seeing him every day. The connection between them had grown stronger as they spent more time together. She had never had a closer friend. Well, Saturday would come soon enough.

Turning on her old laptop, KC put on a kettle of water for some tea and sorted through the pile of mail that had collected while she was gone. Junk mail, junk mail, catalog, catalog, bill. The trash can filled up quickly, leaving just a few bills and one catalog of interesting assorted stuff that she could not resist keeping on the table. The whistling tea kettle sent her rushing the seven short steps to the kitchen. She then emptied the bulging plastic shoebox that Mr. Knitzer had delivered.

Wow! All of this for me?

She opened each get-well card, read it, and placed it on the table in a basket. Then she read each letter.

"Thank you for risking your life to share the last moments of the Iliana Lookout with us."

"I met my husband at the lookout tower nearly twenty years ago. We will always remember it."

"Thank you for sharing your experience—I am glad that you are doing well. I spent one summer at the Iliana Lookout Tower when I was a young girl, during a difficult time in my life, and I am sad to know it is gone."

KC returned the stack of letters to the shoebox, surprised and touched at the personal messages that showed her how much her readers care. She spent the next two hours speed reading though her social media accounts. Mr. Knitzer was right, the number of messages for her was incredible. She was about to answer them one by one, when she came to her senses.

She wrote one single message for each of her social media pages. "Thank you, all of you, for this outpouring of care and friendship. I'm back!"

Time to tackle my email!

There was no way for her to respond to every email, and she knew that most people would not expect it anyway. She glanced at the messages, deleting them as she went. Those from personal friends and co-workers were answered with a quick message. An hour later she had nearly caught up on her email list, when she saw the newest message. It was from Mr. Knitzer's secretary, and invited her to the planning meeting at the newspaper office the next morning. She had never been invited into the coveted planning meeting, reserved for high-level writers, editors, managers and other important newspaper people.

Wow!

That evening, she could hardly wait for Nick's call to share the news with him.

"They probably want to give you a big raise and a cake."

"Maybe they want to fire me and give me a cake."

"Hey, as long as you get cake, what difference does it make?"

***

The morning alarm blared insistently, waking her rudely. She reached over and hit it unnecessarily hard, then remembered the important meeting and jumped out of bed. She had stayed up late researching local events, doing everything in her power to come up with something exciting and newsworthy to suggest for her next column. The best that she managed was a cooking competition for students sponsored by a well-known restaurant. There was also a police incident where a cat had gotten stuck in a sculpture at a local park but she was definitely not going to take on that one.

Walking to work in the morning was one of her favorite things to do. A quick stop at a coffee shop near her house provided her with a high-priced, high-calorie coffee drink, an unusual treat for herself, and she sipped it as she walked as briskly as possible in unfamiliar heels to the newspaper office. Gathering a notepad and pen from her desk, KC straightened her skirt and made her way to the top floor.

I am going to the planning meeting!

THE STORY OF THE YEAR

She was only two minutes late, and no one seemed to notice. They were engrossed in a discussion of the latest scandal from the mayor's office, and Mr. Knitzer was busy handing the assignment to their top political writer. The fast-paced meeting was fascinating for KC, seeing for the first time the work that went into making their newspaper so great. Lost in the chaos and high energy of the conversations going on in the room, she almost missed her cue when the editor-in-chief turned her way and spoke her name. She was prepared to share her idea for the cooking contest, but she was not prepared for Mr. Knitzer's next statement.

"KC, while you have done an admirable job writing 'Around the Block' for the past year, we do not feel that is the best fit for you."

Am I being fired, right here in front of all these important people?

Am I being promoted to the 'Around the County' column?

He continued, "Your columns this past month have been excellent, and our readership has grown as a result. We would like you to keep up the momentum. What would you suggest?" The question was sent out to the room at large.

KC just stared at him for a moment, her look of puzzlement turning to a big grin. She had dreamed of this moment. And here it was. Her chance to really write. Something important.

Don't mess this up!

One of the other editors suggested, "How about going out on active fires with the team that came to your rescue? We could call the column 'Into the Fire with KC Adams'".

Bite your tongue!

"I could write about former lookouts and their experiences through the years."

Total silence.

"George Stripings worked as a lookout at Iliana in the sixties. He wrote 'My Way, Your Way' there."

Mr. Knitzer's face lit up with a rare smile. "Excellent!"

Ideas for names for the new column poured forth from the people in the room. 'Lookout for KC Adams' was immediately dismissed, as was 'Around the Tower', and the tongue-in-cheek 'Fire Retardant'. Someone proposed 'Guardians of the Mountains', which was getting better, but not quite right. They finally decided on the column heading 'On the Lookout with KC Adams' as a catchy and appropriate title. One of the editors mentioned that it would remain suitable for other types of content once this story-line was exhausted. KC beamed with the vote of confidence for her journalistic longevity contained in that simple statement.

The energy from the room was contagious.

"I'll start by contacting the woman who has been the firewatcher there for the past five years."

Nick and she had talked about Jennifer Barco, the woman who had been at Iliana in recent years and had graciously allowed KC to take her place this eventful summer. He had planned to introduce KC to her, and mentioned that she lived nearby, which would help with KC's tight deadline. She was wondering if she could still get it done by Wednesday.

"Your new column will be published in Sunday's paper."

It could not get any better than this!

Wednesday's 'Around the Block' announced her new column and had a fairly flattering photo of KC, followed by the actual column written by the newly promoted obituary writer, Sam Sampson, who unfortunately had decided to write about the cat.

SEVEN

Armed with her shiny new tablet and glowing new confidence, KC rang the doorbell. Nick had been wonderful about arranging this interview with Jennifer Barco.

"Jen has spent her last five summers as the fire lookout at Iliana. Just wait until you meet her! I know you're going to love her!"

"I just hope she likes me."

"What's not to like?"

Just as KC was about to ring the doorbell a second time, a woman that KC had been told was in her late sixties opened the door, tossing her long gray ponytail over her shoulder and waving the huge pipe wrench she was carrying toward the back of the house. "Come in. I'm fixing a pipe in the kitchen. We can talk there."

"Thank you, Miss Barco. I'm looking forward to talking with you."

"Call me Jen."

All thoughts of the stereotypical retired schoolteacher went right out of KC's head. Jen was wearing an old Army tank top and khaki shorts. She padded to the kitchen on bare feet, her toenails polished a modern shade of glittering ice blue. She did not offer tea and homemade cookies, as KC expected from a woman her age. "I think there is some hummus in the fridge, if you are hungry. Grab me a bottle of water while you are in there."

"Sure."

KC took two bottles of water off the refrigerator shelf next to the kefir, and handed one to Jen who was sitting cross-legged on the floor in front of the sink, surveying the work ahead of her. She talked while she worked, and KC typed as fast as she could on the attached keyboard of her new tablet, trying to keep up. When the interview was finished, there was enough information to write two columns.

I just might do that. This stuff is just too good to leave out.

An hour had passed before she knew it, and they had moved from the now repaired kitchen sink area to the living room. Photographs of Jen in South America lined the walls.

"These are amazing photos."

"Thanks. I was in the Peace Corps there for three years. That was the first thing on my bucket list after I retired. I loved working with the families and the other volunteers, but the kids really stole my heart."

"What's next?"

"I'm off to Alaska for a caribou photo experience later this year. Then, who knows. I may just stay home for a bit and write a book about my adventures."

"Let me know if you do that. I would love to read it, and I'll be sure to mention it in my column."

"Cool!"

"Before I go, I have one question to ask you. I found an old, red diary under the bed in the lookout before the fire. Did you ever see it when you were there?"

"Really? No, I had no idea. How old is it?"

"I don't know yet, but I intend to find out."

"Let me know when you do. It will be interesting to see where it came from and when. You might check with Zippy."

"Zippy?"

"He was the fire lookout the year before I started, but he was also the lookout there sometime in the seventies. I think I have a Christmas card from him somewhere with his address."

KC left Jen's house with some great raw material for her column and the contact information for Zippy Roth. She could not wait to share this new lead with Nick.

It was after five by the time the interview was over, so she decided to head straight home rather than returning to the office. It was going to be a late-night sorting through her hurriedly typed notes to begin the draft of her column. Stomach growling impatiently, KC realized that she forgot all about lunch in her excitement with the interview.

I should have accepted the offer of the hummus.

Mentally going through the contents of her almost bare cupboards, she pulled up in front of her apartment. There at the top of the steps, leaning nonchalantly against her door, was Nick, holding a big bag with Chinese lettering.

KC smiled broadly as she climbed the steps. She did not know which smelled better, Nick's woodsy soap scent or the aromas wafting from the bag of Chinese food.

"What a wonderful surprise! Did you hear my stomach rumbling from your place?"

"Yes, I did. The National Earthquake Information Center reported a disturbance in this area."

While she took the food in the kitchen and retrieved plates from the cupboards, a strange, awkward silence fell on her little apartment.

Has a week apart changed things with Nick?

Nick placed his good hand warmly on her shoulder. "I've missed you, KC."

She turned and smiled. "I've missed you too!"

They sat at her little table after she set out the food and poured tall glasses of ice water. It felt natural to have Nick in her home, and she realized how empty it had seemed without him.

Chopsticks clicking, KC and Nick resumed their conversation between bites as if the week they were separated had never happened.

"I can't wait for you to read about Jen. Did she ever tell you about the time . . . ?"

Nick gave her an update on the progress with the fire. "The fire itself is out, they are just starting to mop up. The crew will check out stumps and look for hotspots."

"Well, that is good news. Did we lose a lot of trees?"

"Not as many as we might have. Your quick response in reporting the fire helped stop it sooner than would have been possible without you. You did good!"

"Thank you."

"No, thank *you*!"

Dinner was over, without as much as a bowl of left-over rice remaining. KC and Nick sat down on her little couch with a fresh pot of tea and two of her favorite cups. The old, red diary and the mysteries it contained, lay on the coffee table in front of them.

"Have you read any of it?" KC carefully picked up the book.

"Nope, I just thumbed through it hoping to find a name or a date. Nothing jumped out at me. I spoke to the few guys still in the office and not in the field, but no one there knew anything about it."

"Well, let's do this logically, from the beginning then. We will let the writer tell us her story with her own words."

"Or his own words."

KC smiled, "Perhaps, but the flowery penmanship and sweet introduction speak more of a woman's writing to me. Let's see!"

***

As I sit in my new home on top of the world, with the clouds and the birds as my neighbors, and the flowers and trees as my décor, may the words come easily, and may my heart and soul be calmed by the writing of them.

***

"Ok, I give it to you. Probably a woman." Nick conceded. "Read on."

KC turned the page carefully, finding that the pages were sturdy and the old paper did not seem at all fragile. As Nick had said, there was no date on the page.

***

Last night was my first night here at the Iliana Lookout Tower, and I was able to sleep until morning for the first time in many months. My heart is still heavy with sadness, but the good rest and this quiet, meditative place will heal the wounds with time. Am I running away? Yes, I probably am. I found the highest, most remote place that I could. One without prying eyes and questioning looks. This will be my summer of peace, after a year of chaos and uncertainty. Well, I had better get to work. There are daily tasks to be accomplished, and I am content in doing them.

***

The next page listed some of the duties, which were similar to those that KC had performed. The writer had stood out on the same balcony and scanned the same horizon for smoke, checked in for weather reports, maintained the tower. No mention was made of anything that would establish a timeframe. Nothing really interesting was written there and the words were absolutely no help in finding the answers to the mysterious person who had written them.

"Did Jen know anything about the diary?" Nick asked as KC stopped to sip her tea.

"No, but she mentioned Zippy Roth and thought that he might know. He is next on my list to be interviewed."

"Oh, I met him my first year on the job here. He is a very interesting character. I would love to go with you when you talk with him, if it works with my schedule."

"That would be great! Right now, though, I have to go through the notes I made from my interview with Jen and compile them into an actual column." KC sighed, and looked at Nick who quickly took the hint.

Standing, he pulled KC up into a quick hug. "I will leave you to your work, then. See you on Saturday. Don't read any more in the diary until then!"

"I promise. We will read it together."

KC stood in her doorway, smiling at him as he drove away. Being with Nick recharged her batteries better than the delicious and unexpected dinner. Letting out another little sigh, she went back inside to begin her work.

EIGHT

On the Lookout with KC Adams

July 19

On a quiet day in June, over five years ago, Iliana Lookout Tower was graced with the presence of Jennifer Barco. Just back from a tour with the Peace Corps in South America, Jen was looking for a tranquil place to spend the summer. Little did she know that this mountaintop journey would be repeated for many more years, the experience as addicting as really good chocolate.

Retired after thirty years of teaching, Jen traveled through Europe with friends for a summer. She spent nearly three years in South America, where she taught some very special children, and helped to rebuild a village devastated by a storm. She is not one to sit still. Taking on the position of fire lookout was just another challenge, a challenge that would test her mettle the very first summer.

The tedious part of the job such as cleaning and maintaining the building, hauling water for washing (drinking water is carried in) and regularly reporting on conditions, is coupled with the trial of creating meals from food packed up the long mile hike to the tower. I myself found the latter more challenging than the former, having been spoiled by a mother who is an excellent chef, and by close friends who readily share a pizza or meals at wonderful restaurants. My own cooking abilities are minimal at best. Jen, it appears, can live on oatmeal and peanut butter without any concerns. The silence of this lifestyle can be difficult for some. I asked her how she passed the time. "I spent a lot of hours on the mountain the first year learning Chinese, in preparation for a trip that I was planning the following winter."

THE STORY OF THE YEAR

Nearly a month into an extremely hot summer on the mountain, Jen told me that she awoke to see thick smoke coming from the north. After meeting Jen, and getting to know her, I am certain that she would be calm and professional in any situation. As she talked about her first season on the mountain, and seeing her first fire, she very calmly explained what happened next. She told me that she determined the location and distance and called it in. The winds blew the smoke closer and closer as the day went on, but Jen maintained her composure and stayed at her post, in constant contact with the dispatcher. She remained alert during the entire night, sitting on the little wooden stool and carefully watching the progress of the fire. The next morning the helicopters and planes flew over the area again and again, for the second day, intent on dropping their load on the encroaching flames. By late that afternoon they had finally succeeded in extinguishing them. Her quick actions had stopped a possible disaster.

Tired and dirty from the dust and the smoke, Jen walked part way down the path to a little meadow and the spring where she got her water. She remembers splashing her face in the cold, clear water, and washing off the layers of dirt covering every exposed inch of her body, happy to cool off. Feeling refreshed, she filled her container and headed back up the path. This is where the story gets really interesting.

She left all the doors and windows of the lookout open to allow the breeze to blow in some fresh air. As she grew closer, she heard loud noises coming from inside the building. Ever curious and rarely cautious, Jen boldly walked inside and came face-to-face with a black bear, availing himself of her peanut butter. Thinking quickly, she grabbed a tin of smoked fish that was on the little table next to her, opened it, and began leaving a trail of tempting treats as she backed out of the door. The bear followed. She threw the last pieces of the fish off the steps and the bear lumbered down to retrieve them. She quickly went inside and closed all the doors and windows tightly. She saw the bear, briefly, the next morning at the timberline. As the smoke dissipated, the bear disappeared also. "It was an unforgettable summer," Jen said of the incident.

Thus ended the excitement of her first year at the lookout. She would repeat this for five more years, and goes on record as the last lookout there.

I have some more exciting stories to share with you as we travel together back in time to learn the history and mysteries of the Iliana Lookout Tower.

Until next week,

KC Adams

***

The next morning KC turned her completed column in to the newspaper and spent the rest of her morning on the phone trying to reach Zippy Roth. She finally left a voice message and hoped that he would return her call.

The afternoon went by quickly, spent on research. A quick call to Nick at noon broke up the long, boring day of documentation and research.

"What are you doing?"

"Paperwork. What are you doing?"

"Paperwork."

"I miss you."

"I miss you too."

She ended her day going over a satisfying list of updated contact information for the people who had been lookouts at Iliana, that Nick had provided her.

The second column, inspired by the copious notes that she had taken during her interview with Jen, practically wrote itself. Now a week ahead, she was determined to wade through the copies of the fact sheets that Nick sent to her from their archives. After all, she was not writing a novel. As a journalist, she wrote interesting stories based on facts. She absorbed information on the building of the lookout and the dates of various updates. She looked at faded photos. She added names to the list Nick had given her and spent hours tracking down information for those people that she could find.

As the days passed, she spoke with Nick every evening. She found herself rushing home in anticipation of his call.

"How was your day?"

"Long, boring. I hate computers. I hate paperwork."

"Hmm. Personally, I love computers. I am finding out so much about the people who used to work at Iliana."

"I'm glad you're having fun."

"Don't be grumpy."

"Is that the way you talk to your friends?"

"That's what friends are for, to cheer you up and to point out your faults."

"I don't have any faults."

"Oh, that's right. I forgot. You're perfect."

"Yes I am."

But not perfect for me.

KC sighed.

She had not heard back from Zippy Roth, and had arranged instead to talk with Karen Brownsville the next morning, a woman who had been a lookout during World War II and was now living in a retirement home on the edge of the city.

"I am seeing Mrs. Brownsville tomorrow. Do you want to come with me?"

"I am so envious! I would love to come with you, but I have a dumb meeting I have to go to. I hate meetings even more than I hate computers." Nick grumbled. "I always wanted to meet Mrs. Brownsville. She had quite the reputation for being a feisty and tough young woman in her days as a lookout. Did you get the newspaper article I found for you in the archives?"

"Yes, thank you so much! I wish you could join us, but I understand how much work there is this time of year."

"Yeah."

KC avoided talking about the fact that Nick was still stuck on desk duty when his heart was in the field with his team. Deep inside, she was pleased that he was working somewhere safe instead of being out on the fire line, where she knew from experience, danger lurked around every corner. She could not bear to lose such a close friend.

And Nick was just a friend, as she assured her mother on every phone call. Her own heart beat just a little faster each time she said it, like it does when you tell a little white lie and know inside that it is wrong. But she ignored it and just kept repeating the mantra to herself "just a friend, just a friend". She could not risk falling in love again with a man who jeopardized his life with every new assignment. She would guard her heart carefully this time.

"Are we still on for Saturday morning to read more from the old diary? My curiosity is killing me!"

KC laughed. She had just barely managed to avoid the temptation of reading further in the diary on her own. They had made a pact over tea and fortune cookies that they would do it together. "Come by at nine and I'll toast you a bagel."

NINE

KC entered the assisted living home carrying her computer tablet and a flowerpot full of pink miniature roses.

"I am here to see Karen Brownsville," she announced to the young woman at the front desk. The woman barely glanced up from the novel that she was engrossed in to tell her the room number.

The lobby was full of people talking animatedly about the latest book on the bestseller list. At a large table to the side, several women put together a puzzle while discussing the attributes of a well-known and handsome male actor. The music playing in the background was not the quiet classical score that she anticipated, but rousing tunes from the 1960s. Yes, there were walkers parked here and there, but the atmosphere was not at all what KC had expected.

Walking down the hall, she noticed decorations on the doors, each reflecting the occupant's personal taste. One had red-white-and-blue flowers with an American flag pinned above it. Another bore an opulent wreath of pink and purple silk flowers.

She rounded a corner and found the room number the receptionist had given her, the door bearing an elegant spray of simple white baby's breath dried flowers.

"Come on in."

"Mrs. Brownsville?" she called as she entered the lovely room. The walls were decorated with seascapes framed in whitewashed wood, glassware in shades of blue and green sat on the side tables, and pillows in cool pastels accented the plush white chairs. Pots and vases of flowers where everywhere, and KC did not know if the lovely scent that filled the room came from the flowers or the occupant.

"KC Adams?" A woman dressed in a flowing caftan in shades of royal blue and purple came into the living room from the back. Her white hair was piled artistically on her head, she wore gold hoop earrings, an assortment of bangle bracelets, sparkling gold slippers, and just a touch of pink lipstick. "Just call me Karen. Please, sit down."

"Thank you, Karen." Juggling her tablet and the flowerpot, KC managed to hand her the roses before sinking down deeply onto the soft chair.

I hope I can get up out of this chair.

Opening her tablet, KC smiled her most professional smile and began the interview. "I am here to ask you about your time as a fire lookout at Iliana Tower."

"Yes, Dear. So you said over the phone. What is your name?"

"KC Adams." This was not a very good start, if Karen Brownsville had forgotten her name that quickly.

"I know that, Dear. But I cannot call you KC. It is not at all suitable for such a lovely young woman. What is your given name?"

"Kerry," she replied with a smile.

"Much better! Well, Kerry, what would you like to know?"

Three hours later KC left the building with some amazing stories of Karen's time as a fire lookout, as well as in-depth knowledge of a very full, adventurous, and satisfying life directly from the lips of a vivacious ninety-something year old woman. This included the details of seven (yes, seven!) husbands, assorted children, grandchildren, great grand-children, and even great-great-grandchildren.

When she got into her car, KC checked her phone and saw a text from Nick. "Was it amazing?"

"Good thing you did not come or you might be husband number eight." That ought to keep him smiling for the rest of the day. She would tell him all about it on their call that evening.

For now, she was anxious to return to the office and type up her next column while the facts and the essence of Karen Brownsville were still fresh in her memory.

***

On the Lookout with KC Adams

August 2

I am so pleased to be able to share with you the story of an amazing woman, who lives right here in our city. Karen Brownsville was the fire lookout at Iliana for three summers starting in 1943. She was in her late teens at the time, and had married her high-school sweetheart, Ronald, before he enlisted in the Army and left for Europe.

Athletic, strong-willed, and determined, Karen was one of many women who stepped into jobs previously held by men before the war. It took a strong woman to haul her own water, chop her own wood, cook what food she had been able to pack, while manning the tower to look for fires, as well as to be a spotter for possible enemy planes.

Karen shared with me the details of one such day in her life as a lookout.

"I got up before dawn to chop wood and light the fire. Coffee and tea were rationed, but I managed to stretch out the coffee grounds I had by reusing them for several days. Breakfast was often crackers and canned cheese, or occasionally oatmeal. I would warm water for a quick wash-up, but a full bath was out of the question. I also had no facilities for washing clothes, and I imagine that by the end of the summer mine could have stood up and walked out by themselves. After looking carefully through my binoculars for any sign of smoke, recording the temperature and humidity, I checked in over our new two-way radio, as I did every half-hour. We were one of the few stations with the new radios, which were mainly reserved for the military, however the old telephone system was not reliable so far up the mountain. I would then walk down the steep path to a little meadow spring to fill up my containers with enough water for the day. I also would check my traps for small animals to supplement the mostly dried and canned food

that I subsisted on each day. A pot of squirrel stew was a rare luxury. On one quiet morning, as I was hauling water up the path, I heard a small airplane approaching from over the mountain. I dropped the water and sprinted back up the path, my heart racing from the exertion and the fear. The chart on my wall confirmed it. The plane was a Japanese Zero! I called in the sighting immediately. The supervisor came on the line to congratulate me on correctly identifying the plane, which had been captured and was being flown by our own people. I was glad to have been correct in my identification, but angry that they thought it necessary to test me in such a heart-stopping way."

A newspaper article from 1944 hailed Karen and several other women as '. . . courageous women and girls who have stepped into a man's job under lonesome circumstances.'

I asked her about the isolation and loneliness I myself had experienced even for the short time I was in the tower. I know that you are also wondering how someone could be cut off from seeing other people for many months, and choose to repeat that experience for three years. Here is her answer.

"My husband and thousands of other brave men were fighting a war against tyranny and oppression, against aggression and unspeakable acts of murder, against the powers of evil men with evil intentions. Every day they risked their lives so that we at home and our allies abroad would be free, would be safe. Compared to that sacrifice, what hardship is there in carrying water or wearing dirty clothes? What is a little loneliness? I was a strong young girl, and that experience and those that followed made me into a strong woman. I bore five children and buried seven husbands in my long life. If I had the strength and stamina today, I would go back to my mountain again. I would watch the sunrise and remember."

And we will remember you, Karen, and those like you who stood watch over us and our forests in the Iliana Lookout Tower. We wish you many more sunrises.

Until next week,

KC Adams

TEN

The alarm went off promptly at eight on Saturday morning, but KC was already up and in the shower, anticipating Nick's arrival. She shut off the annoying, high-pitched sound as she dried her hair and slipped into her comfortable weekend outfit of worn jeans and a soft T-shirt. Tying on her old running shoes, she made her way down the stairs with a light step and headed around the corner to buy fresh bagels. When she returned, she found Nick waiting on her doorstep, a full half-hour early, wearing a similar outfit and a big grin.

"Good morning, KC. I knew you would be up early. You are just as anxious as I am to read that diary."

"Good morning!" Offering him a quick hug with her free arm, she opened the door and set the bagels out on the table along with two cups of coffee that she had brewed. She needed something stronger than tea to keep her focused this morning.

They sat comfortably side-by-side on the couch, ignoring the enticing smell of the fresh baked bagels in their urgency to find out what else the old red diary had to offer.

"I have been good all week. I did not even peek at this book."

"I'm proud of you. I'm not so sure I could have resisted just a quick look. Are you ready?"

"Ready."

KC opened it carefully to the third entry, holding it so that they could read it together. The previous page had held a simple list of the duties of a fire lookout. The next page was similar, and Nick reached for his coffee and took a bite of his bagel, prepared for a disappointing and boring morning. The following page had him sloshing his coffee back onto the table and leaning into KC to read what had been written.

***

I am a vile and wicked woman, and what I have done can never be taken back. And yet I would do it again in an instant. What does that say about me? Can I view my sin with such dismissal and say in my heart that I would do it yet again if I could achieve the same outcome? Up on this mountain there are no distractions to keep my mind from focusing on the events of the past year. I did it, and I am paying the consequences of my actions as I sit alone in this little wooden tower and remember.

***

"She killed someone and buried the body." Nick offered.

KC kicked him playfully in the shin. "You are here to help me solve the mystery of the fire lookout who wrote this. You are not here to turn this into a murder mystery."

"We will see. Turn the page!" Nick placed his good arm around the back of the couch and rested his hand on her shoulder in order to lean in closer to the diary.

***

I woke up today thinking of Henry. Poor Henry. I may have buried his body, but his memory will live on in my heart forever. Well, enough of this. I have work to do.

***

"See! She buried the body! I told you."

KC just poked him in the ribs with her elbow, and turned the page to find yet another list of duties accomplished, and sighed.

"Boring. Where is her confession and the location of the secret grave?"

"You read too many mysteries."

"Well, yes, I love to read mysteries. I take offense, however, at your last statement. You can never read too many."

They took a short break to eat their bagel breakfast and drink their coffee. Nick moved away from her to gain the use of his good arm to eat with, and she missed the warmth. When the bagels were reduced to crumbs and a second cup of coffee poured for each of them, they resumed their previous positions on the couch to continue reading, and KC was again enveloped in his warmth. She smiled as she turned to the next page.

***

I was thinking of Henry again today, and remembering his red hair and crooked smile and sweet nature. Our love was not something to be ashamed of; I am coming to understand that as I spend my hours alone. Perhaps I should have waited. Yes, I know I should have waited. Yet we did not wait. That one night of sharing our love was beautiful, despite my guilt. Had he lived, Henry and I would have been married right away. But it was not to be, and so I must resign myself to the consequences of my actions, even though they were the result of such a love.

***

"That is so sad!" KC said, wiping a tear from the corner of her eye.

"Yeah, no murder there." Which earned Nick another kick in the shin.

"Well, if we are trying to find out who this is, we need to get a timeline. The fact that she feels guilt for sex outside of marriage probably puts it back quite a few years, I'm sorry to say. It is such an accepted activity in this day and age." KC sipped her coffee thoughtfully.

"Unless she was a Christian or a woman of strong faith, and that is why she felt the guilt." Nick reached over and flipped to the next page. "Let's see what she has to say next."

The following pages were again lists of duties performed. One such entry caught Nick's attention. "Wait, go back to that again. She mentions fetching drinking water. Let's write down some facts. Do you have a notebook?"

"I am a reporter. Of course I have a notebook." KC rummaged around in the center drawer of her little desk, and came back with a small notebook and pen.

Nick took them and jotted down a note about drinking water as he explained. "The Iliana has provided fresh drinking water for years now, since the spring water is not completely safe to drink. So let's see if we can find out when that change happened."

"Now you are thinking like a detective. Or a reporter. What other clues can we find?" KC picked up the notebook from the coffee table where Nick had placed it, and began to write down a few of the other facts they gleaned from the lists of duties.

The next personal entry appeared several pages later.

***

I cried myself to sleep last night. An unfamiliar animal called out from the darkness and it sounded just like a little baby. The sound produced such anguish in me that I could not stop sobbing. I crossed my arms over my empty body and remembered the child I carried there. I am alone. Empty and alone.

***

Nick hugged KC closer as she reacted to the words with tears. "She lost a child. The love-child of Henry, who died. Two deaths in the span of a single year."

Wiping her eyes with the back of her hand, KC turned to the next page, and sat up straighter as she read the words written there.

***

I held her for just a moment, but I loved her. I call her Sara in my mind, although I do not know what the family who adopted her named her. She will always be Sara to me. She wrapped her little hand around my finger and looked at me with Henry's blue eyes and red hair, and my heart broke. I loved her too much to keep her, to have her live under the cloud of being born from a mother who was not married. Of course, Father was quick to point out the shame it would cause our family as well. I saw the way those in our town looked at me as my belly began to swell. The heavy, over-

sized coats did not fool them, especially as the weather turned warm. Even when Father sent me away to live with my Aunt, the knowing stares followed me whenever I ventured out. How could I put that shame on my daughter? No, she is better off with a real family. But I will never be the same again.

***

"So the baby did not die! Still, it is so very sad."

"Yes it is. But there's nothing we can do about it," Nick said with a sigh.

KC looked at him for a moment, and her mouth turned up in a big grin, lighting up her entire face.

"I know that look. We are in for trouble."

"What if we can track down the child she gave up for adoption and reunite them? It is much easier to open adoption records than it used to be. It could change her life. And it just might be the story of the year!"

"Hold on there, Miss Reporter. First of all, we have no idea when this diary was even written, or if the woman who wrote it is even still alive."

KC's expression changed in an instant. Nick could not bear to see her looking so disappointed after the smile she had flashed at him just moments before.

"Maybe we don't have the answers yet, but we can figure it out, if we work together."

"Yes! It may not be a murder mystery, but it is a mystery. Let's see what we can find."

They spent the rest of the morning combing through the next pages of the diary for any other facts that could help them. It was after two when they reviewed their list, not even a quarter of the way through the journal. They did not have a lot yet, but perhaps enough to get started. Nick's stomach growled loudly enough to elicit a grin from KC and initiate the call to order a pizza.

After making short work of their lunch, they opened the notebook and reviewed the notes on the table in front of them and divvied up the assignments for the week.

"OK, I have several things that I can look up this week, since I'm stuck at my desk anyway. First, when they started packing in safe drinking water. Also, she mentioned a small five-acre fire on the fourth of July just north of the lookout. I will comb through the archives and see if there is any record of it."

"Good! And I will question Zippy Roth when I meet with him on Wednesday. You are welcome to join me if you can break away from your desk."

Nick gave her a scathing look and then winked. "Very funny. I'd be happy to join you on Wednesday. I'll postpone my pencil sharpening duties until Thursday. Be sure to pray about this. God has a way of working things out for our good and that of the writer."

How long has it been since I've thought about praying for something like this? A long, long time.

Nick gave her a quick hug and left her standing in the doorway smiling.

ELEVEN

Wednesday dawned hot and muggy, a typical August morning. KC dressed in her favorite blue cotton interviewing outfit and sandals, then headed to her car for the trip south to meet Zippy Roth. She was picking up Nick on the way, happy that he had managed to get the day off. When she found herself whistling on the way there, she made a determined effort to tone down her attitude and turned on some quiet music in the background instead. She convinced herself that the joy she was feeling was all about meeting the famed lookout and hearing his story, and the possibility of learning something that would lead her closer to finding the writer of the diary. It had nothing, absolutely nothing to do with spending the day with Nick.

KC had never been to Nick's house before, and was surprised to find it nestled in some tall fir trees at the end of a cul-de-sac in a family neighborhood. For some reason, she had expected a bachelor to live in a modern, no-nonsense apartment with a pool and a gym and no lawn to mow. She found Nick waiting on his front porch.

"Nice place!"

Their conversation flowed easily as KC drove the scenic road to the next town.

"I asked a retired dispatcher to go through the records for me to find out about the water and the small fire. Ruth loves stuff like this. She will find the answers to our questions and anything else that might help."

"What a great resource! Tell Ruth thank you from me."

KC did not know what to expect from this interview. Nick explained that Zippy had a reputation for flirting with the women, for staying at his post through an intimidating forest fire, and for shooting a cougar when it threatened a hiker. They rode in companionable silence listening to music and enjoying the views. That was one of the special things about being with Nick. Neither felt the need to fill up the silence with meaningless chatter. At the same time, they could talk about anything and everything with ease.

As they approached the small town, KC asked Nick to verify the directions.

"It is just up here about two miles, on the right."

They drove past Main Street, past the businesses, past the schools, and into the industrial area. Just as KC was sure that they had missed the street they were looking for, they found it. The old building had been freshly painted, and the landscaping was surprisingly vibrant in this dusty part of town. KC gathered her purse and tablet and they headed upstairs to the address they had been given.

"Are you ready?"

"Yes, ready and excited. I heard from Jen that Zippy has a lot of stories."

"Did she also warn you about him?"

"Warn me?" Just then, Zippy Roth opened the door and promptly gave KC a big hug and a kiss on the cheek. Her eyes grew wide with surprise at the affectionate greeting from a total stranger. Nick would have come to her rescue, she was certain of it, if he had not been trying so hard not to laugh. As he ushered them in to his living room, KC had a chance to take in the details of the room and then focus on the man himself. The room was blue. The walls were blue. The carpet was blue shag. The couch was a blue crushed velvet. The room was in perfect coordination with Zippy himself, who was wearing a light blue leisure suit, an outfit which KC recognized from seeing one in an old James Bond movie. His shaggy hair was that reddish color that is achieved with some of the products that promise to cover gray. His long sideburns, which had not accepted the hair color so readily, were white.

"Mr. Roth, it is a pleasure to meet you," KC finally said as she sank onto the blue couch.

"Call me Zippy" he said with a wink. "The pleasure is all mine." Wink, wink.

Grateful for Nick's presence by her side, KC had managed to avoid sitting right next to Zippy, much to his dismay. James Taylor was singing love songs quietly in the background. KC hid her grin as she perceived that Zippy's plans had been totally ruined by Nick.

Once past the awkward beginnings, Zippy shared some terrific experiences from his time at the Iliana Lookout Tower. While Nick encouraged him to talk asking specific questions, and kept him from straying into non-relevant stories, KC typed as fast as she could on the detachable keyboard for her tablet. By the end of the session she had collected the fascinating and numerous stories from the 1970s that Zippy remembered. He had been the lookout for eight years, and he remembered everything in great detail. He had returned to the lookout for one summer just six years ago, and had some very interesting things to say about the small changes that had taken place in the thirty years since his previous experience.

KC made notes of the changes not just for her column, but for the research that they were doing on the woman who wrote the diary. As she and Nick questioned him, two facts stuck out. They brought drinking water to him in the seventies. And he had not noticed the diary under the bed during his time there.

Frankly, a child outside of marriage was becoming common place in the 1970s, as it is today, so the anguish portrayed in the diary would not be likely. At least it gave them an indication that the diary was written well before Zippy was a lookout.

"Thank you so much for your time. You shared some amazing experiences, and my readers are going to be thrilled to read about them."

"Are you sure you can't stay longer?" Zippy held her hand tightly.

"No, I'm sorry. Deadlines, you know."

Managing to extricate her hand from Zippy's determined grasp as she said goodbye, KC headed back to her car and the peaceful ride home.

"Why don't you stay for dinner?" Nick asked as they grew closer to his house. "I make a great omelet. Or you could have my second-best dish, chili dogs."

KC smiled, and accepted gratefully. "I'm sorry that I have not been much company on the drive home. I was composing my next column in my head while it was fresh in my mind."

"No problem. Just being with you anywhere is nice, even in the silence."

Warning! KC chided herself. There was nothing the least intimidating about that statement. Friends liked being together. And Nick was just a friend.

Dinner was perfect, a tasty veggie omelet and her favorite chocolate chip mint ice cream for dessert. The conversation was lively, as they commented on the stories that Zippy had shared, and laughed at his flirting with her in his vintage seventies apartment.

"Are you sure you don't want to replace this boring hardwood flooring with a nice, blue shag?"

"I'll keep the oak, thank you."

"You are a surprisingly good cook, Mr. Evans. Thank you for dinner, but I really need to head home now."

"I know. You are a busy woman. I need to make it an early night anyway. Those pencils won't sharpen themselves tomorrow!"

KC promised to share her column with him as soon as she had it finished, and headed for the door. She smiled, and leaned into him for their usual hug. And then it just happened. The kiss. Not just a little, friendly kiss. A peck on the cheek. A mere touch of the lips. This was a KISS. A toe-curling, breath-catching, unforgettable, once-in-a-lifetime, fireworks-inducing, perfect first kiss.

Pulling away determinedly, KC backed slowly toward the door and mumbled something inane, heading toward her car as fast as her shaky legs could carry her. Confusion gave way to anger as she recalled the self-satisfied look on Nick's face as she made her retreat.

TWELVE

"Let me get this straight. You are angry because a totally gorgeous, wonderful, smart, sexy, fire fighter, who incidentally saved your life, kissed you?"

KC looked up at Carol, the woman who sat at the desk across from her at the office.

"You don't understand. We are just friends." KC listened to the whine in her voice and broke out laughing.

Amanda stood up from the other side of the partition separating them and joined in. "Yeah, KC, you may have to re-evaluate that."

No, even if it sounds crazy, I cannot fall in love with Nick. The risk of losing him is too great.

Just then the phone rang, and it was George Stripings' agent. The famous writer had worked as a lookout at Iliana in the early sixties. He wrote his first bestselling book *My Way, Your Way* there. Getting this interview was pivotal for KC, since she had brought it up during the meeting where she was given this new column. Luckily for her, he was about to release a new book, and the agent could not arrange an interview quickly enough. Unfortunately, George Stripings was now living in Los Angeles. She hated doing Skype interviews, but it looked as if that would be necessary this time. Agreeing to get right back to the agent, KC got into the elevator and headed toward Mr. Knitzer's office. To her surprise, she left with approval to fly to Los Angeles for the interview.

Her plane landed without incident, and KC found a taxi to take her to her hotel. The hustle and bustle of the huge airport was energizing, just as she had envisioned when she thought about traveling to faraway places in search of the next great story. It had been her dream in college. Since Derrick's death in a plane crash, she had not ventured anywhere farther than a car ride away. She had just settled into the hotel room when her cell phone rang.

"Hello, Nick, how are you doing?"

"I'm fine. I was just thinking of you in that big city alone."

"I'm not alone. I'm surrounded by millions of caring people."

"Yeah, right. Anyway, I just wanted to wish you well on your interview tomorrow and to tell you that I miss you."

"Thank you, I miss you too."

"Good night. Get some sleep."

"I will. Good night."

I will not. I'll toss and turn dreaming of you and wishing things could be different.

Leaving her hotel the next morning with her tablet in hand, KC caught a taxi to the address the agent had given her. She did not know what she expected, but the posh condo was not it. Mr. Stripings had not wasted the money from his bestselling books. After ringing the bell and being buzzed in, she found herself in a lobby appointed with white leather furniture and modern glass tables topped with crystal lamps. Emerald green walls against a light golden marble fireplace suggested a scene from the Land of Oz. A frazzled-looking man in his late fifties, with thin graying hair and tortoise-shell glasses, rushed up to her, introducing himself as George Stripings' agent. He briefly shook her hand and urged her toward the elevators. The elevator stopped at a high level, but not quite as high as the penthouse unit, and the agent hustled her down the hall to the door. After ushering her inside, he just as quickly left her there, shutting the door decidedly behind him. KC looked around at the beautifully and professionally decorated room, so perfect and spotless that she hesitated to go all the way in and just hovered in the entryway.

"Come in, come in my dear. Sit right here next to me." George Stripings appeared from a back room dressed in perfectly pressed khaki pants and a starched blue shirt. She had seen photos of him on the dust cover of his books, but she was shocked to find him looking nearly the same, although it had been more than fifty years since the first of his books were written. His black hair was just as dark as ever, and though obviously not his natural color, it was still thick and a bit longer than the usual modern cut. It was his face that surprised her the most. He had very few wrinkles for a man who must be in his mid to late seventies. As they sat down and he attempted a smile, she understood that the reason was not the fountain of youth, but some talented plastic surgeons and likely a good dose of Botox, based on his tight expression.

He deftly slipped his arm around her on the back of the couch, and KC smiled as she remembered a similar interview with Zippy just the week before. She found herself wishing that Nick was there, partly to act as a bodyguard, and partly to share the incredible view of the city from the window. She rose and went to the window, commenting on the beautiful building and the lovely view. When she returned to the couch she managed to sit farther away, facing George, as he asked to be called, and placed her backpack and tablet on the couch between them.

The interview went amazingly well. George had a clear, precise memory of his time at the Iliana during the summer of 1961. He talked a little of the duties that he had, and briefly of a small forest fire caused by a careless camper that had been quickly extinguished thanks to his own actions. Mostly he talked about writing *My Way, Your Way* during his long, hot summer there, and his struggle to get it published over the next year. He also told her about the other books that he had written since then, though none were the classic that his first book had become. He also surprised her by telling her that he had read her columns before agreeing to this interview, and he encouraged her to continue to write. He plugged his new book, as she expected, and she agreed to mention it prominently in her column.

There was nothing new in the information that he shared that cast any light on the mystery woman who wrote the diary, except the mention of how comfortable the built-in bed had been. KC politely refused his offer of lunch, saying that she had an early evening plane to catch.

On the flight home, she attached the keyboard to her tablet and typed up the interview, deciding to run it in her next column and putting Zippy's column after that. Zippy had shared so much that he had provided enough information for several columns, so she now had three weeks covered.

Even though it was late by the time she returned to her apartment, she returned Nick's call after listening to her voice messages.

"Is everything OK?" she asked.

"Sure, why wouldn't it be?"

"Well, we spoke last night, and I noticed that you left me several messages on my answering machine. I thought it was urgent."

Nick hesitated for just a moment. "I just missed you. Things are fine here. Hey, how about meeting halfway for dinner tomorrow?"

KC paused for just a millisecond before accepting. The KISS may have changed things, or perhaps it had not. She just knew that she missed Nick and could not wait to see him. Yawning, she headed for her own comfortable bath and bed. She could sort out her feelings tomorrow. She would review her column on George Stripings and tweak a few things before sending it in the morning.

***

On the Lookout with KC Adams

August 9

I am happy to share with you all the story of an American icon, George Stripings, who was a fire lookout at the Iliana Lookout Tower in 1961. I had the honor to meet with him in Los Angeles this week. As timeless as the books he is famous for writing, decidedly youthful and articulate, I found myself in awe of both the man and his surroundings.

Rising toward the sky, high above the crowds in a luxury condominium, George Stripings lives and writes in a lovely home with an incredible view of the city below. His newest book, **The City Never Rests***, takes place in just such a location, he told me, and is expected to be released later this month. I have no doubt that it will join his other works on the shelves of many readers such as yourselves.*

I asked him about his time at the Iliana. "It was a hot, dry, quiet summer. I was young and inspired by the beauty around me and the peaceful life of a fire watcher. I wrote My Way, Your Way during that long, lonely summer. The words just poured out of me, onto the pages. The secluded, isolated, serene environment of the lookout tower allowed the characters to come to life without interference. It was an author's dream job."

George Stripings was as much of a hero that summer as the lead characters in his books. He told me of waking one morning to the sight of smoke, rising from the base of the mountain not far from the lookout. He called in the report immediately, but he did not wait for the fire crews to respond. He slung the pack that he used to carry water from the spring onto his back, grabbed a shovel, and made his way on foot down the mountain, right into the path of the smoke. He found a frightened camper there with a campfire built improperly on open ground, littered with dried wood and leaves. The fire had spread from where it had originated and was crawling toward the unprotected forest nearby. The camper was madly hitting at the fire with his sleeping bag, succeeding only in fanning the flames. George Stripings jumped in and doused the fire with the water that he carried, then used the shovel to cover the remaining coals with dirt, effectively smothering any residual embers. By the time the fire crew arrived, he and the camper were sharing a much earned can of cold soda.

I am personally looking forward to reading The City Never Rests as soon as it hits the shelves of my favorite bookstore. And I will never forget my meeting with George Stripings, fire lookout, author, and gentleman.

Until next week,

KC Adams

THIRTEEN

KC looked at her watch again, tuned down another refill on her water, and tried not to turn her head toward the door yet again. It was not like Nick to be late. The nagging little voice inside her asked the ever-present question. "What if something has happened to him?" Just like Derrick. From someplace in her memory, a Bible verse came to her. 'Do not be anxious for anything . . .' She could not remember the rest, but just that little bit was comforting.

She felt the warmth of a hand on her shoulder, and looked up to see Nick smiling down at her. "Sorry I'm late." He placed both arms around her and gave her a quick hug before taking his seat at the table across from her, grinning.

Both arms?

"You got your cast off!"

"Just came from the doctor, which is why I was late. I wanted to surprise you."

They ordered quickly, the conversation flowing smoothly as it always had before the KISS. Perhaps KC had built the situation up to more than it had really been. She was lost in her own thoughts, and almost missed what Nick was saying.

"I will be going back out into the field in just a few weeks, and I can tell you I will not miss that stupid desk one bit!"

Back into the field. Back into danger. KC's stomach tightened and her breath grew shallow, as she tried to smile and congratulated him.

"What's wrong?"

"Nothing is wrong. I just thought that you would be out of the field for the rest of the summer."

Someplace nice and safe, like your desk.

"Yeah, I did too. What can I say? I heal quickly. I'll be glad to get out from behind that desk."

"I'm happy for you."

"You don't look happy."

"I just worry about what might happen when you are out on a fire."

"Hey, I am a firefighter after all, and not an accountant. It's what I do."

"I know. I just wasn't quite ready."

Nick gave her a puzzled look, and shrugged his shoulders as he dug into his salad.

Try as she could, she could not remember a single word of that comforting Bible verse. The nagging voice was winning. "Be careful. Don't fall in love. It is dangerous."

After another hearty hug from Nick and a promise to get together on Saturday to delve into the rest of the diary, they each went their own way.

The next day, KC worked from home and typed up two columns from her interviews with Zippy. She was not happy with either of them. When Nick called that evening, he could hear the frustration in her voice.

"I thought those columns would write themselves. How can you run short of words for a character like that?"

"Well, you write it then!" KC was immediately contrite. "I'm sorry, Nick. It has just been a tough day for me."

"Do you want to talk about it?"

"No."

"Did you have dinner?"

"Oatmeal."

"Yum! Do you still want me to come over tomorrow for our Saturday diary marathon?"

"Yes, of course. I think I will just call it a day and try again later." KC shutdown her laptop and stood up, stretching her cramping legs. "I look forward to seeing you in the morning. Really."

"I'll bring breakfast."

KC tossed and turned into the early morning hours as she struggled to come to terms with her feelings for Nick and her fears. She managed a short prayer.

"Dear God, take care of Nick when he's out there. Don't let him die." Somehow those few words made her feel better, and she fell asleep.

The sunlight poured in through the open window, bringing with it the smell of gasoline and exhaust from the mechanic's shop next door. The air was already hot. KC rubbed her eyes and looked at the clock. Nick was due to arrive in just a few minutes. She threw off the sheets and took a three-minute shower, wrapped herself in a towel and brushed her teeth and dried her hair at the same time, an amazing feat that she had learned in college.

When the doorbell rang just a few minutes later, she answered with a look of nonchalance that defied the hectic rush of the morning she had endured so far. Nick stood there with two bags bulging with groceries, and another sending out the enticing aromas of breakfast sandwiches and hot coffee.

"What's in the bags?"

"Just a few things to fill your pathetically empty shelves."

"I am totally capable of shopping, you know."

"I know. Just say thank you."

"Thank you."

"You are welcome. Ready for breakfast?"

"Oh, yeah!"

Satiated and caffeinated, KC felt ready to tackle the diary in earnest, and let the nagging concerns about the rest of her life fade into the background.

"I think our big problem is that we are both too analytical. We keep stopping our reading of the diary to solve the mystery without fully understanding the entire picture."

Nick placed his arm along the back of the couch behind her shoulders and she was so distracted that she almost missed his reply.

"I was thinking the same thing! Today we read the entire diary from cover to cover."

"Let's give it a try."

A quick review reminded them of the list of duties that the writer had listed, and her heartbreaking admission of having a baby she called Sara. *How could I put that shame on my daughter? No, she is better off with a real family. But I will never be the same again.*

"OK, so she was not married, she had a baby girl, she put her up for adoption." KC restated the facts thus far, more to get herself back into the substance of the writing in the old diary than to remind Nick. She reviewed the rest of the notes quickly.

He picked up the book and turned to where they had left off and began to read.

***

I thought of Father today as I washed the windows all around the lookout. What would he think of his oldest daughter doing menial work? Yet there was such satisfaction in the glow of the glass as I surveyed the results. I know he does what he thinks is right for us. I could not help but wonder what our life would have been like if he had been a simple construction worker or a mailman. Having such wealth can be a curse as well as a blessing. I also wonder what direction I might have taken if Father had a son. The burden of being expected to take over his business one day would have fallen on him instead, and my future would be my own. I envy my sister, and her ability to be such a free spirit. Father does not always approve, but he does not have any expectations of her. Sighing will not change anything.

***

KC made a few notes about wealth and a family business, and Nick read the next entry in the diary.

***

Several young men came today to deliver food and supplies, and brought mail addressed to me. I tried to act nonchalant, but the fear in my eyes must have shown, because the tall one gave me a very strange look when he left. Perhaps I am just oversensitive. How can a letter be addressed to me in the name I used for this position, when it is not even my real name? Who would know to do that? I opened it with shaking hands, and then sighed with relief to find it was from my dear friend Kathryn, the only one who knew of my plans to come here.

I will not write back, as I'm afraid it will give me away. I will try to visit her when I leave the tower at the end of the summer. Father's career can't take this scandal, and I can't take his wrath if he should find out where I am. He believes that I am in Europe with my sister. I will leave it at that. I have chores to do now.

***

Nick stretched his legs out and rubbed KC's shoulder, causing her to jump up and head into the kitchen to refill her nearly full coffee cup. Nick followed closely behind her, taking the nearly overflowing cup from her hand and placing it back on the counter, then turning her around to face him. "We need to talk. Ever since you kissed me, things have been strained between us."

"I kissed you! As I recall, you were the one who kissed me." She placed her hands on her hips and glared at him. And then it happened. Again.

He kissed her. And she kissed him back.

Nick smiled down at her with a self-satisfied expression and gently moved a lock of hair away from her forehead. She looked up at him, slightly dazed. Then she raised up on tiptoes and planted a big kiss right on his smirking lips, and their expressions were reversed.

"Better?" he asked.

She kissed him once more just to be sure. "Better. Let's get back to the diary."

Nick led her back toward the couch, and they picked up the book and sat down as if nothing had happened in the interval.

"New information here. She is from a wealthy family. And even if we manage to find out her name, it will not be her real name."

"You have so little faith in my writer's sleuthing abilities." KC poked him playfully in the ribs. "Read on."

***

> Yesterday was so exciting! There was a fire on the mountain just to the east of the lookout tower. When I awoke, I checked in every direction with the binoculars, as I always do. And there, curling over the tops of the trees, was the smoke. I used the fire finder as I was taught, and called in the fire location over the radio as if I had done it for years. The fire crew responded immediately, being nearby working on a bridge. It had spread to just ten acres when they finally got it under control. They credited my quick reporting of the fire for keeping it that small. It seems that a family with eight children had managed to set their little tent on fire along with the brush and trees around it. No one was hurt, thank goodness. I felt so very proud, since I have only been a firewatcher for such a short time. I may only have this job for this one summer, but I will always remember that I was able to help.

***

KC picked up the little notebook and added to their list of facts the information about the location and size of the fire, the comment about the family with eight children, and the fact that the crew was working on a bridge. It was not much, but they both thought that the facts as a whole would help them hone in on the year the diary was written.

***

> This morning I woke up with some renewed determination to do something with my life. This past year, with the loss of Henry and the humiliation surrounding the birth of the

baby, and my need to give her up, I have had my self-esteem beat down to nothing. I took this position as a fire lookout to run away from the world, to hide out and immerse myself in my own pain and loss. Spotting that fire and reporting it, then seeing so many of my beloved trees saved as a result, has renewed my faith in myself a little. The sadness is not gone. It never will be. Little Sara is six months old today! Yet a new sense of hope has filled some of the empty spaces.

One of the firefighters brought me a Bible as a thank you. Today I read Philippians 4:6-7 'Be careful for nothing; but in everything by prayer and supplication with thanksgiving let your requests be made known unto God. And the peace of God, which passeth all understanding, shall keep your hearts and minds through Christ Jesus.' My faith in God is renewed. He has forgiven me my sins. He holds my future in His hands. I will trust in Him.

***

There it was! The verse that had eluded KC. Could she accept it just like that? Could she allow herself to fall in love with Nick, knowing that he put his life in danger every time he went out on the fire line? The thought was so tempting, with him sitting right there beside her with his arm around her shoulders. She wondered if she would feel the same once the reality of his career choice set in. Would she be willing to risk suffering loss for the sake of love?

I don't know if I can.

"Earth to KC." Nick poked her gently on the arm. "I was asking if you wanted to go to church with me tomorrow."

KC thought just for a moment. "I am going home tomorrow for a few days. I can finish my column from there. In fact, could we put aside the diary for today? I really need to pick up a few things and pack."

"You are going home without me? How will you ever manage to eat your mother's famous Sunday cinnamon rolls all by yourself?"

They said goodbye at the door with a friendly hug, and agreed to meet again the next Saturday morning to finish reading the diary.

THE STORY OF THE YEAR

KC made it home just in time for church on Sunday morning. She listened carefully for the first time in many years. Her heart was not fully opened yet, but she was not completely shut off either. The pastor spoke about Daniel as a young man, and the tests he faced for his faith in God. KC had only one test in her life and she had failed it miserably. No, that was not right. Derrick's death led to a failure of her faith. The fire, however, had not. She had called out to God in her race down the mountain. She still had time to let that test produce a stronger faith. She was not ready to fully embrace that thought right now, but she was willing to consider it.

After a quick lunch, KC went into her father's office and immersed herself in the work of re-writing the two columns on Zippy Roth.

***

On the Lookout with KC Adams

August 16

I have the privilege of introducing you to a true icon of fire lookout history. Zippy Roth presided over the mountains and valleys surrounding the Iliana for nearly a decade in the 1970s. He shared with me, on a recent interview, his love for the mountains and the joy he felt as he manned the Iliana Lookout Tower for so many years.

He was a true trail-blazer. No, really! If you find yourself hiking in the vicinity of the Iliana Mountains, you just may be walking on a trail constructed by Zippy himself. He had a dream of opening access for people to see the beauty that he encountered every summer. With the permission of the local Forestry Service, he worked each spring with a mostly volunteer crew to create those access trails.

It was during one of those hard-working late-spring evenings, when most of the crew had gone home for the day and Zippy was working with two other men to finish the last quarter mile of trail that it happened. As the darkness descended and the light grew dim, he still worked feverishly. He paused just for a moment, and in the silence, he heard rustling in the nearby brush. He peered into the bushes, and saw two glowing eyes looking back at him. And then, as brazen as could be, the big cougar came out onto the trail behind him and challenged his right to be in her territory. She growled. Without a moment's hesitation, Zippy started the chainsaw that he was holding which growled back. The cat looked a little perplexed at first, but when Zippy revved the motor, she yielded to the louder growl and ran off into the darkness of the forest. The two men with him that evening told the story, and Zippy became a legend.

From blazing trails, to protecting the forest that he loved, Zippy Roth was a modern day mountain man. He constructed benches around the lookout tower from wood scavenged in the area. He dug out a section below the local spring to create a makeshift bathtub. He hunted for his food, cooking squirrel and quail and any other game that he could catch or shoot.

Many fires were stopped thanks to the quick response to their smoke, as Zippy watched over the land from Iliana. He received his reward in more than just the monetary payment a lookout is entitled to for the hard work he or she performs. The Forestry Service honored him with their highest award two years in a row, for enriching and for saving the forest he loved.

Zippy Roth, still as vibrant as he was when he sat on top of the mountain those many years ago, is working on writing his memoirs. This reporter is looking forward to reading the stories of this amazing man and his time spent in the Iliana Tower.

Until next week,

KC Adams

***

The second column practically wrote itself, as KC shared the stories of Zippy and his adventures. As she went through her copious notes, she chose to leave out the many references to the women who visited him at the lookout tower. He would probably include them in his memoirs, if he ever actually wrote them. He was a character, and she would never be able to look at anything reminiscent of the '70s again without thinking of him.

Just as she finished sending the columns off to her editor, Nick called.

"Miss me?"

"Maybe, but I am sitting at Dad's desk eating a Sunday cinnamon roll that I want to keep all for myself. What did you have to eat today?"

"I don't want to talk about it. I just wanted to tell you that I had a nice phone conversation with my boss yesterday afternoon. He knows of a couple who worked at Iliana during the 1950s. I called Susan Johnson, and she is more than happy to talk with you. Can you meet with her on Thursday? I've emailed you her contact information and address."

"Yes! That would be wonderful. Thank you so much! Do you want to come with me? Assuming you can get off of work, of course."

Nick was silent for a moment. "I have been released to go back into the field. My team is heading into Idaho tomorrow. We've been assigned to the Two Rivers fire that got out of control yesterday."

"Oh." KC's hand went to her chest in an attempt to control her racing heart. It did not help.

"I'll miss you."

"I'll miss you too. Please be careful!"

"I will."

They said goodbye without the usual banter, and KC pushed her cinnamon roll back onto the plate, and tried to think positive thoughts.

FOURTEEN

KC stretched and smiled as she saw the familiar walls of her old bedroom light up with the rising of the sun. She was up early, surprising considering the amount of sugar she had consumed the previous day. She could have stayed in bed for several more hours.

Dressed in her oldest and most comfortable jeans and a sweatshirt, KC headed for the kitchen and a cup of tea and perhaps just one more cinnamon roll. Her father had beat her to it.

"What brings my daughter here at this early hour on a Monday morning?"

"Is that the last one?" KC asked.

Her father cut the cinnamon roll in half, and carefully looked at the two pieces, deliberately taking the largest for himself. It was an old game, played out over countless pieces of cake and sweet rolls and leftover pie. "So what brings you here?" he repeated.

She understood the question, but was not ready to answer just yet. "I just wanted to see you guys and finish my column in a quiet, uninterrupted place. I miss you, Dad!" A hug and a kiss on the cheek did not convince him, but he let it go at that.

A short time later, as she sat in the office, responding to her emails and messages from her loyal readers, KC heard her father leaving for the hardware store, as her mother hummed and washed the dishes in the kitchen. Familiar sounds in a familiar place. The comfort and security of being home.

After finishing the surprising amount of emails, and responding to the equally amazing number of social media communications addressed to her, she walked into the kitchen and put on the kettle for another cup of tea. Settling down into a comfortable chair and leaning her elbows on the table, she asked her mother if she wanted any help. Mom just smiled and said that she had it all under control. As she always did.

A few minutes later she hung up the dishtowel, poured herself and KC a cup of the freshly brewed tea, and sat down beside her daughter.

"So what brings you here?"

"I think I'm falling in love with Nick, and I don't want to."

"Uh, huh. I can understand why a girl your age would not want to fall in love with a sweet, smart, handsome firefighter who obviously adores her."

KC just gave her mother an exasperated look, and was about to explain her feelings when the doorbell rang.

"Hold onto that thought, I'll get it."

A few moments later, Mom came back into the kitchen escorting Geoffrey. He came over and awkwardly patted KC on the head before taking a seat at the table and accepting the cup of tea that her mother offered. After laying out a plate of homemade cookies, which seemed to be in never-ending supply, her mother excused herself to check on the laundry and left them alone in uncomfortable silence.

Geoffrey seemed totally oblivious.

"I just stopped by on my way back from a house call. A checkup for a beautiful Doberman and her ten puppies."

"That's nice."

He then mentioned that he would like to have a dog himself someday soon, which turned into a conversation about buying a house, and then grew dangerously close to a conversation about the two of them buying a house together.

KC squirmed in her seat and tried to come up with any excuse to flee the scene. Where was her mother? Just then the kitchen door opened and Dad came into the room. Was KC's sigh of relief audible?

"Well, hello Geoff! How goes the business?"

Geoffrey responded that his practice was doing well, which led to the suggestion from her father that perhaps he should return to his office in case someone needed him.

"Thank you!" KC rose and gave her father a peck on the cheek. "And where did you disappear to?" she asked her mother as she came back into the room.

"I thought you two might want to be alone. If you do not want to fall in love with Nick, what is wrong with Geoffrey? After all, he is a doctor!"

"He's a veterinarian!" KC and her father responded in unison.

"Is that what this sudden visit is all about?" her father asked. "Are you and Nick falling in love? Cool!"

"It is not cool." Mom spoke up. "She said that she does not want to fall in love with Nick."

"Well, then, she should definitely consider Geoffrey." Dad smiled and winked as he said it, but her mother did not seem to get it.

"Why not? You could live in a nice house, close to us. He is a nice young man."

"Yes," added her father. "We could set up a nice little office over the hardware store and you could write nice articles for women's magazines on important issues like how to make the perfect turkey, or organize your closets."

Mom, finally understanding what was taking place, jumped in with enthusiasm. "You could come to Sunday dinner every week, and join me at the semi-annual book sale for the library. Wouldn't that be nice?" She winked at Dad, smiled and leaned back with her arms folded across her chest, proud of herself.

Both of them just looked at KC and waited for her to explain when she was ready.

I'm ready.

"I had it easy as a child. You kept me safe and protected. Our church was an extension of family for me. My faith in God was never in question. Now, I'm just not sure."

"We worried about you when you went off to college."

"Oh, I did just great in college. I kept my distance from drinking and drugs, I stayed away from anything you taught me was wrong."

"Then, what happened to your faith?"

"I fell in love with Derrick. He was the ONE for me. I planned our entire future in my head. And then God let him die."

"You blamed God?"

"Yes, I blamed God. I did everything right—why did He punish me like that?"

"Oh, Honey, God did not punish you." Her mother moved her chair closer and held KC's hand."

"Yeah, yeah. Bad things happen to good people."

"Yes, KC, they do. We live in a fallen world, not a perfect world." Dad's voice was soft. "Is that why you are afraid of falling in love with Nick?"

"Yes! I mean, he is a firefighter. He puts his life at risk every time he goes out on the line. If I fall in love with him, I could lose him, just like I lost Derrick. I can't go through that again."

"I don't think you have a choice, KC. I think you're in love with him already."

"No, I can fight it. I will not be in love with Nick. Period."

"You can't blame God for everything that goes wrong in your life, KC. We have all been through difficult times, and without our faith, we would quickly fall into despair, or worse yet, turn off our hearts so that we no longer even care."

"You can't possibly understand what I went through with Derrick. I mean, you have each other. Except for losing Grandma a few years ago, and that was expected, you have not had to go through a loss like that."

"We should tell her, Mary," her father said in a quiet voice.

"Yes, Ken, it is time."

Tears flowed as Mom told her of a brother born several years before KC. A brother who lived just a few weeks. Dad told of holding him in his arms for one last time, and then giving him up to God. Her father quoted 2 *Corinthians 1:3-4* '*Blessed be God, even the Father of our Lord Jesus Christ, the Father of mercies, and the God of all comfort; Who comforteth us in all our tribulation, that we may be able to comfort them which are in any trouble, by the comfort wherewith we ourselves are comforted of God.*' That's a mouthful, but it means that God comforted us, and we can comfort you. Someday you will be able to console another."

"If we had given up on having children because of our loss, you would not be here." Mom hugged KC and passed the tissue box.

By the time they left the kitchen, KC had at last been able to let go of her grief. She had finally given her heart back to the God she had trusted as a child, praying with her parents right there at the kitchen table.

"Lord, I'm sorry that I backed away from You. I know that You never left me, even though I turned my back on You. Please, be patient with me. I believe in You, with all my heart. Thank you for Your grace, Your love, and Your steadfastness."

Her faith in Jesus restored, she thought of Nick. She would not be afraid. She would let love happen.

Heading to her room for a short nap before dinner, KC found herself lying there fully awake. She mulled over the anguish of her parents losing a child, and thought of the incredible sorrow of the young mother who wrote the diary. She was determined more than ever to help find the mysterious woman and reunite her with her daughter.

I know you are out there somewhere.

FIFTEEN

Bright and early on Thursday morning, KC made her way through the traffic of the city, trying to avoid the gridlock of rush hour. Once safely on the outskirts, she stopped at a little café and had a strong cup of coffee and a veggie omelet. She was not even tempted to try the pancake special, having consumed enough sugar over the weekend to last her until Christmas.

Reviewing the information she had printed out on the location of the Johnson house, she typed the address into the GPS app on her phone. Her old car had no such amenities. She ate a leisurely breakfast, biding her time so as not to arrive too early. She knew that older people liked to sleep in, and guessed that Jason and Susan Johnson were no exception.

Arriving promptly at nine-thirty, KC pulled up in front of a charming cottage in a lovely neighborhood. The house was painted a pale butter yellow, with the quintessential white picket fence. She closed the gate behind her and headed toward the unexpectedly bright, lime-green front door.

Susan Johnson answered on the first ring, dressed in jeans and a flattering navy blue flowered top. Her red hair was cut short and little brass bells jangled at her ears when she walked. She led the way to a modern and comfortable living room, where coffee and cookies were set out on the table. KC's stomach rebelled at the sight of the sugar cookies, covered in a thick layer of frosting with multi-colored sugar sprinkles on top. She politely took one and set it on a napkin beside her tablet.

"I want to thank you and your husband for taking the time to see me."

"Jason is not with us, I'm afraid."

"Oh, I'm so sorry! I didn't know." KC flushed red with embarrassment to have gotten her facts wrong.

"No, no dear, he is not dead! He is just playing golf." Susan Johnson laughed.

The conversation was lively and belied the fact that the woman was in her mid-eighties. KC had already compiled pages of good interview material on her tablet when Jason arrived from playing golf. Dressed in khaki shorts and a lime green polo shirt that matched their front door, he gave his wife a kiss on the lips and a little pat on the knee as he snatched a cookie off of the table and joined her on the couch.

Grinning, KC asked a few more questions. "So you worked together as fire lookouts at Iliana from 1950 through 1960. George Stripings took over the lookout in 1961."

"No, that is not quite right" Jason spoke up. "Remember, Susan, we took the summer of '55 off to go to Budapest."

"Oh, that's right. That was the year that nice young girl, Jane Johnson, took over for us. We thought it was funny that she had the same last name. I don't think it was her real name though."

That statement had KC's full attention. "Why did you think that it was not her real name?"

"Oh, we asked her if she was related to some of the Johnsons we know, and as we listed them off she seemed very uncomfortable and changed the subject," Jason answered.

Susan added, "She was a sad, tiny little thing, barely over five feet tall I would guess, and a bit frail I think. I remember how pale her skin was."

"Can you tell me any more about her?" KC asked.

"Well, she had blonde hair and big, green eyes. She did a fine job of taking care of the tower while we were away. We visited her again at the end of the summer when we returned, and could see that the sun and wind of the mountain had brought a little color to her cheeks."

Jason continued, "We asked her to come back and visit us on the mountain if she was ever in the area, but we never saw her again."

KC told them about the red diary that she had found, although she did not reveal the contents. They both agreed that it could have belonged to Jane Johnson. Then they shared a very important fact. When they began to work at the Iliana Lookout Tower in 1950, there were only a few folding cots for sleeping. The bed where she had found the diary had not been built until 1953.

Thanking the couple for a wonderful interview, KC promised to email them a copy of the column as soon as she had finished it. They were heading to Italy the following week with a tour group, and did not want to miss reading it.

When KC returned home, she practically threw her tablet down on the table as she rushed to call Nick and share the news with him. The call went straight to voicemail.

"Nick. I can't wait to tell you about my interview with the Johnsons. I think I found our mystery diary writer! I miss you. Please call me back."

She typed up her notes into a more readable outline, finding that she had enough information for two very good columns. She also pulled out the little notebook and added to the list of facts that she and Nick had pulled from the diary. The woman's fake name had been Jane Johnson. She had manned the tower in 1955. She was a small woman with blonde hair, green eyes, and pale skin. There was no proof that this Jane Johnson was the woman they were trying to find, but KC felt sure that she had found her. Or at least found out about her. Actually finding the real woman would be another thing altogether.

Just before she went to bed, KC tried Nick's phone again. Voicemail. The little nagging voice returned, but she replaced it with a prayer. "Please, Lord, keep Nick safe and bring him back to me soon."

The following morning, KC verified that her phone was turned on and in her pocket before she left for her office. She checked it just to be sure several times that morning, and by noon, she decided that he was just out of cell range. By that evening, she began to worry.

The next morning, KC followed the same routine, checking her phone often until lunchtime, when she gave in to her concerns and called the Forestry Station where Nick worked. She was patched through to a co-worker.

"I know that Nick and his crew are working on the big Two Rivers fire in Idaho, but I wondered if there is a way that I can reach him. No, it is not urgent. Yes, I'll hold."

An hour later KC walked into her apartment and carefully put down her backpack. She got a drink of water, then sat down on the couch. And cried. And prayed.

Nick's boss, James, whom she met briefly after the Iliana fire, had told her that Nick's team was trapped behind the fire line and had been out of contact for several days. He assured her that they were doing everything they could to get control of the fire in that area and find the team. Nick was the best, he reassured her, and they would find them safe, and soon.

KC turned on the TV and turned to a twenty-four-hour news station. A few minutes later, they had a brief update on the Idaho fire, including photos of a plane dropping retardant on some angry flames. She turned off the TV, realizing that watching was not going to help.

KC slid off of the couch and down onto her knees. "Lord, please save them. Do not take Nick from me. I know that You love him, that he is Your child. I trust You with his life, and with mine."

She stood up feeling surprisingly calm. Making her way into the kitchen, she made herself a snack of cheese and crackers, and a comforting cup of her favorite tea. She set the plate and cup on the table in front of the couch, and opened her tablet, planning to work on her columns on the Johnsons. She had accomplished little writing the previous day. Her eyes were drawn to the Bible sitting on the edge of the table next her, a fine layer of dust coating the burgundy leather cover. The cheese got warm and the tea grew cold as she spent the next several hours reading God's Word. Such security and comfort were contained within those pages. How had she spent so many years ignoring this book? She found herself praying effortlessly, as if talking to a dear old friend. She knew that whatever happened with Nick, she would not walk away from God again.

KC looked up a Bible verse that she remembered from her Sunday school days. *Proverbs 3:5 Trust in the LORD with all thine heart; and lean not unto thine own understanding.*

I trust you, Lord.

The phone rang, jarring her out of the peace of the afternoon, the cheerful ringtone an unexpected sound in the quiet of her deep thoughts and prayers. She picked it up and heard the good news from the familiar and welcomed voice. "Thank you, Lord!" she shouted out loud.

Nick sounded exhausted, but safe and sound. "We took shelter in a nearby cave and waited out the fire unsinged. Remember the experience I told you about, when my crew leader, Wayne, saved us? I had the chance to do the same for my crew."

"I prayed for you non-stop."

"God must have listened."

"God always listens."

"Yes, He does, even when His answer is 'no'. I'll be heading home tomorrow. I can't wait to see you!"

She hung up with a huge smile on her face. Nick was coming back to her. She recited the verse that she had just read a few minutes earlier, *Psalm 118 O give thanks unto the Lord; for he is good: because his mercy endureth forever.*

SIXTEEN

The donuts smelled so good it was all KC could do not to sample one, or at least sneak a little of the maple frosting, but Nick was due to arrive soon. She walked away from the kitchen and the temptation. The last two columns she had written on the Johnsons had been proofed several times, and sent off to the paper, and her small apartment was as spotless as possible. Unable to sleep in anticipation of seeing Nick, KC had been dusting at six that morning. She glanced at the diary again, waiting on the coffee table, but kept her promise and did not open it.

He's here!

KC opened the door and practically jumped into Nicks arms as he approached her door.

"Whoa! I am happy to see you too, but can we hug inside?" Nick pulled her back into her apartment and shut the door before giving her a long hug and a sweet kiss.

"I missed you."

"I can tell! I missed you too, KC. But I'm here now. You can let go of my arm so I can get the circulation back." Nick smiled and KC melted.

I love you.

She did not say it out loud.

"Is that coffee I smell?"

Seated in their usual places on the couch, with nothing left on their plates but donut crumbs, Nick picked up the diary and opened it to where they had left off.

KC referenced the little notebook. "Here are my comments from my interview with the Johnsons. Jane Johnson, the name she gave herself when she was a lookout, was at Iliana in 1955. Blonde hair, green eyes, just over five feet tall."

"That is a huge discovery, KC. Good job!" Nick held up his hand for a high five.

"Let's see what else we can find."

***

I was awake half the night reading my new Bible. I have a peace in my heart that has eluded me until now. Thank you, Lord!

Today I ventured down to the little spring, humming an old hymn as I went. Squirrels and birds chattered their own songs as I made my way down the path through the trees and brush. And there it was, standing just a few feet in front of the spring, big and intimidating and menacing. My heart pounded in my chest, but I did not back down. I am a purple dragon, after all. Who was this big, furry, creature to challenge me? I waved my arms and shouted "This is my water! Go away!" The raccoon took off running and I have not seen him since.

***

"OK, that was funny. Weird, but funny. Why does she think she is a purple dragon?"

"You got me there. Write it in the notebook. Maybe it's a clue."

The next few pages were simply comments on the day-to-day tasks of a fire lookout.

"Oh, here is something good." KC continued reading out loud.

***

This life is so different for me, that I am surprised at how well I am doing. Father has pampered me and my sister so much. I never appreciated the people he pays to cook and clean for us until I had to do those jobs myself. I will never again make such a mess in the kitchen, knowing how much extra work it creates for those who have to clean it up. My old nanny, Margie, tried to instill a work ethic in us when we were children, but neither my sister nor myself listened. Perhaps if Mother had lived.

I am about to prepare dinner from a can of beans, some spices, and some macaroni. It may not be the gourmet food usually served at home, but I am making it myself. It is my second try at this dish, and this time I will add some extra chili powder. I wonder sometimes, if life had given me different circumstances, would I have been a good cook? I remember winning that cooking contest in my home economics class in school. Was that just a few years ago? Father was not impressed. He could not understand why I was interested in learning something that someone else could so easily do for me. He told me that people with money were different. I almost listened to him when he asked me to change that class for world history. Almost. He is very good at lecturing. And I almost always give in to his wishes. I told him that I would join the debate club instead, and he was appeased.

***

KC jotted a note in the notebook. "They were very rich, she was in school just a few years ago, so we are closer to getting her age. She had a nanny named Margie, and her mother died."

"I'm not sure the name of the nanny will be of much help."

"I'm just being thorough."

"Yeah, yeah." Nick turned the page.

***

I had some visitors today. A couple from the nearby town came up on a hike and made the trip up the steep path to see the tower. The young man carried their toddler on his back in a baby carrier. The little boy was adorable, but it was all that I could do to keep from crying. The man did not look at all like Henry. His hair was dark, not red. And he was quite tall, where Henry was not much taller than me. Yet the sweet family served to show me what I might have had, and lost. When they left I indulged myself in a short cry, but my duties called and I dried my eyes and returned to the tasks at hand. I'm pacified with the thought that somewhere my little girl is loved by just such a family.

***

"Monday morning, I will be back in the office and I will contact Ruth. She is the unofficial historian, even though she has been retired for many years now. If anyone can find some leads for us from 1955, it will be Ruth."

After a prolonged hug, KC reluctantly let go of Nick and watched him walk down the stairs to his car.

SEVENTEEN

The message to come to Mr. Knitzer's office at nine on Tuesday morning came three different ways. KC had an email meeting notice, a written message left on her desk, and a voicemail on her cellphone.

Uh-oh. This is either something very good, or very, very bad.

Tea in hand, tablet powered up and ready, KC adjusted her skirt and headed for the elevator leading to the top floor and the managing editor's office. The door parted with a startling *ding*, and opened to reveal Nick.

"I'm sorry, Nick, I don't have time now. Can you wait until after my meeting?"

"While I'm happy to see you, that's not why I am here. I have been summoned to the same meeting."

"This is weird."

"I know."

The door closed and they rode the elevator up together in tense silence.

"Come in, come in. Coffee? Darlene, get them some coffee."

Seated opposite Mr. Knitzer at his large and rather intimidating desk, KC smiled as Nick squirmed like a kid being called before the principal.

"You are probably wondering why I have asked you here."

KC caught Nick rolling his eyes and kicked him under the table, eliciting a sharp "Ow!" and a contrite look.

This is my job on the line here.

"KC, your stories about the former fire lookouts have been very nice, very nice. Lots of good feedback from our readers."

"Thank you. I have really done my best to . . ."

"But according to our recent polls, and the number of social media responses, the popularity of your column is beginning to wind down. People are becoming bored."

"Sir, I am working on another really good story, but it's not ready yet."

"Hmph. That's good. But if a story is not ready, it's not a story, is it?"

KC felt Nick's foot touching hers under the desk, and she managed a shaky smile. This was not going well.

"I have an idea for the perfect follow up series to your current columns. Actually, my wife had this idea, but I agree completely."

Okay, this is getting stranger by the moment.

"We want to send you around the country to other fire lookouts. You will visit one each week and do a story on it."

"Why am *I* here?" Nick could not hold his question back any longer.

"Ah, Mr. Evans. May I call you Nick?" He did not wait for an answer. "Nick, I have spoken to your supervisor and the head of public affairs for your organization, and they agree that accompanying KC on this tour of other fire lookouts would be good publicity."

"You expect me to go along with KC?"

"Your expertise in firefighting will go a long way to making the stories interesting and accurate."

Dismissing Nick's incredulous response with a wave of his hand, the editor turned back to KC. "The thing is, KC, our readers seem more interested in your relationship with your hero firefighter than the history of the Iliana. You two are an item, are you not?"

KC blushed an embarrassing shade of hot pink, and Nick squirmed uncomfortably in his seat.

"Ah, good, good. We will be sure to get photos of you together at the different lookouts. I will, of course, be sending a photographer along with you." As if noticing Nick's discomfort for the first time, Mr. Knitzer added. "The newspaper is covering all expenses, of course."

A light knock on the door interrupted the meeting, and Darlene admitted a young woman with a big smile and an even bigger camera.

"Come in, come in. KC, Nick, meet your photographer, Ginny Olsen."

Nick broke into an unrestrained laugh, which garnered another kick to his shin under the table, before KC rose and politely greeted the young woman. Nick stood as well, and controlled himself as he shook her hand.

"Just call me Ginny." Her freckled face broke into a grin. She was tall, with her dark brown hair pulled back into a no-nonsense ponytail, and her athletic build showing off muscles that defied the weight of the camera. "We can dispense with the Olsen part, if it's okay with you."

"Ahem! Good, good. Well, you leave for Washington state in the morning." With that sudden proclamation, Mr. Knitzer ushered them out of his office. Darlene handed each of them their airline tickets, itinerary, and contact information. A moment later they found themselves standing by the elevator.

"I've got to call my boss."

"I've got to go home and do laundry."

"This is gonna be fun! I'll go get my camera bag."

EIGHTEEN

The flight to Seattle was so fast that KC had received her orange juice and read only a few pages of the book she had shoved in her purse, before the two flight attendants quickly collected the plastic cups, and the plane began to descend again. They had an hour layover at Sea-Tac, where they grabbed a quick snack, and then boarded another quick flight to Yakima. The last-minute tickets had them sitting apart from each other, allowing no opportunity for conversation.

"I'll get the rental car while you two wait for the luggage."

Ginny and KC nodded their approval.

"My camera bag goes with me." Ginny climbed into the back seat with her precious camera, folding her long legs effortlessly.

KC and Nick grinned at each other as he drove to the hotel. This assignment may have been forced on them, but no one was complaining. Time alone together would be wonderful. A chance to renew the closeness they had established at Iliana.

"You know, this could be a lot of fun."

"Probably not the assignment part, but being with you changes everything." KC reached over and stroked Nick's cheek, and he responded by clasping her hand.

"Pay no attention to me." Ginny laughed from the backseat, and Nick released her hand quickly.

Lunch at the hotel coffee shop was quick, and they all poured back into the rental car to head toward the mountain. Rising above the Cle Elum area was the Red Top Lookout. It was a fairly easy two-mile hike, with beautiful views along the way. Ginny's camera was never still. When they reached the lookout, she had KC and Nick pose several times.

"Smile! You two do not look happy."

"Duh!" KC muttered under her breath. Nick laughed and Ginny snapped the photo.

"OK, that was much better. Can I get a kiss?"

Nick walked toward Ginny and to her surprise, gave her a kiss on the cheek. Then he held out his hand toward KC and they made their way around the lookout, taking in the amazing views.

"That's not what I meant." Ginny called out to their backs.

The day was clear and warm, and they counted five different mountains as they made the circle. Children ran through the door ahead of them as several families joined them inside the small lookout. KC pulled her tablet out of her backpack and managed to corner the volunteer for a quick interview. It was a hectic afternoon, and KC found herself missing the quiet solitude of Iliana. Gathering up the printed brochures about Red Top, the three made their way back down the mountain. Nick stopped here and there to pick up an agate or a piece of jasper, and Ginny paused to take some photos of the view as the sun began to set. KC found herself inexplicably impatient. The mystery of the diary was foremost on her mind. What a story that would be if she could figure out the identity of the writer! This current assignment was not her idea of exciting.

Relax, will you?

Nick caught up with her and reached for her hand. "What's wrong?"

"Not a thing." She squeezed his hand and finished the walk down in quiet contentment.

Following a quick dinner at the hotel coffee shop, they each returned to their own rooms. The next morning KC was up, showered, dressed and packed before dawn. Waiting for the others in the hotel lobby, she worked on the column for the Red Top Lookout.

Exciting place to visit, my foot. How can I lie like that?

"Stupid column!" KC muttered under her breath.

"Having problems?" Nick set his bags down next to hers.

KC managed a smile. "My heart is just not in this story. It sounds like a travel brochure."

"Red Top Lookout, built in 1952, was fully restored in 1997, and is still in operation today. The trail up to the top was short, and we found ourselves with an incredible 360 degree views of the Stuart

Range, Teanaway Ridge, Chelan and Entiat Mountains, and Mount Rainier. The volunteer who manned the lookout that day, had the added duty of providing tours and information for the many visitors who joined us on our hike to the mountaintop."

"Yes, there is not much of a personal touch that you can get from this quick trip. If we could stay longer, talk to some of the firefighters who have worked in this area, you would have something to work with."

"Yeah, like that is going to happen."

Just then a man who looked to be in his early seventies walked up, and Nick turned to him with a big smile followed by a bear hug.

"KC Adams, meet Fred Meeker. Best firefighter in the state of Washington."

An hour later, Nick walked Fred back to his car while KC finished typing up the last of an amazing interview.

"Hey, no one woke me up. We are going to be late for the airport!" Ginny came down the steps grumbling.

"Here, have a bagel and some coffee. Nick is getting the car right now." KC was still grinning as they headed toward the airport.

The plane ride back to Portland was a mirror image of the one to Washington the previous day. Up, down, up, down, home.

"I'll see you at the airport on Monday, Nick," Ginny called as she hailed a cab from the airport.

KC turned toward Nick. "I'll see you on Saturday! The red diary mystery still awaits."

Nick reached out, catching KC's hand. "I can't wait until Saturday to see you. Can we have dinner tomorrow?"

KC pretended to think it over, then gave Nick a dazzling grin. "Can we meet at the same place? Six-thirty?"

When KC arrived at the office the following morning, she found Ginny, Carol and Amanda standing around her desk, looking at photos. She cleared her throat and they all jumped back.

"Just a friend," Carol called as she made her way across the aisle to her desk.

Amanda just snickered.

There, in black and white, were photos of Nick and KC holding hands as they stood against the view from the lookout, one of them standing arm-in-arm on a bluff at sunset, and another looking at each other like lovesick teenagers with the lookout in the background.

KC groaned. "You have got to be kidding." She pulled out a photo with the volunteer standing between them, taken from inside the Red Top Lookout. "This one."

"We'll see. Mr. Knitzer said that he wants to choose the photos for this story, so get to work on that column!"

KC had been so inspired by her interview with Fred Meeker, she had roughed out the column right after arriving at her apartment from the airport. She pulled out her jump drive and transferred the story to her work computer. By lunchtime the story and the photos were on their way upstairs.

***

On the Lookout with KC Adams

September 20

We climbed up the two-mile trail to the Red Top Lookout, built in 1952, and fully restored in 1997. Still in operation today, the lookout affords an incredible 360-degree view of the Stuart Range, Teanaway Ridge, Chelan and Entiat Mountains, and Mount Rainier. The volunteer who manned the lookout that day, had the added duty of providing tours and information for the families who joined us on our hike to the mountaintop. The sky was clear and blue, the sun bright, and the breeze lovely.

While we saw not even a hint of smoke on our excursion, this lookout is one of 30 that are still in use in the state of Washington during the summer months.

I had the great honor of meeting Fred Meeker, a pioneer in fighting forest fires in the state of Washington. In 1962, he began as a fire lookout on North Mountain. While others enjoyed their summer lookout duties in comfortable wooden or steel structures, Fred's home base was a simple tent. He told of hot days and bone-chilling nights spent around a campfire, where he also did his cooking. He shared a story about one such summer night.

"I was cooking a bean and squirrel chili over the small fire, one of my favorite dinners. I had taken the critter earlier that day, and was pleased to have something that was not dried or canned. It was just getting dark, when I heard some rustling in the bushes below me. I was used to a lot of different noises, which always seem louder at night. I reached for my 30/06 rifle, which was never far away. The rustling got louder, and I stood with my back to the fire, ready for anything. Cougar? Bear? There was movement! Out came a big, scary, dangerous skunk. Followed by three little baby skunks. They meandered through my camp, pausing at the bowl of chili that I had set down on the ground. All four helped themselves to my dinner, then waddled their way back down the mountain. I now call my recipe Skunk Chili. No one ever even tries it when I offer, but that's okay. Leaves more for me."

Fred went on to fight fires in a thirty-year career, and is still involved as a volunteer today. The stories he tells of the many fires he has helped control are a testimony to the hard work of the men and women who protect our homes and our valuable forests.

Next week I am off to Nevada, to the Ella Mountain Lookout in search of yet another story, and another adventure.

Until next week,

KC Adams

NINETEEN

KC arrived at the restaurant just moments behind Sam, who was just getting out of his truck.

"Hug?" Sam asked as KC joined him at the entrance. They did not notice the woman behind them snap a photo with her phone.

"Good day?"

"It was okay. Back at the desk." Nick groaned and looked so distraught, KC could not help but laugh.

"You'll survive."

"If I don't die of boredom."

KC felt her heart tighten in her chest. Just the mention of dying, even as a joke, still induced panic.

I've given it all to You, Lord. Haven't I?

Their food arrived and KC relaxed and let herself enjoy just being with Nick. The dinner was lovely and uneventful, and they were both renewed, just having spent time together.

Saturday could not come fast enough for KC.

***

She set out her home-made muffins and made a pot of coffee. Laying out the diary on the table in front of the couch, KC looked out of the window again.

Nick is coming! Is this what love feels like?

"Come in! Breakfast is ready."

"I'm impressed. You made these?"

"I am Mary's daughter, after all."

"Yeah, we'll see." Sam took a big bite of a warm muffin, and gave her a thumbs up as he reached for a second.

KC slapped his hand as he reached for the diary. "Keep your sticky hands off of that! I'll get it."

***

Today I spotted a fire. Well, not the fire, but the smoke. It was quite a long distance away, but I called it in. They said that they are burning some areas that have been logged, to clean the area up and prepare the ground to plant more trees. They apologized for not letting me know. I actually remember hearing something about that when I first got here. It seems that I need to pay more attention to my job, and less time focused on my problems.

My birthday is next week. I am supposed to be celebrating in Paris with my sister. I have no way to contact her, but she agreed to cover for me this summer, and I am sure when Father calls, as he does every year on my birthday if I am not at home, she will find a way to alleviate any suspicions on his part. He is so busy now that he is a senator, I am not sure he will even remember.

***

"Now that is a big clue. Senator."

"Yeah, but that could be federal or state."

"Still, it is a great clue." KC wrote it down.

"You know, we haven't talked about what we are going to do if we find out who this woman is."

"When we find out."

"Okay, when."

"I'm working on it. I want to find the daughter and reunite them."

"That is sweet, KC. It will depend on both the mother and the daughter wanting to be reunited."

KC dismissed the thought with a wave of her hand. "Of course they will."

"Hey, let's put this aside and go for a walk. It is a shame to waste a beautiful day like this indoors."

The afternoon was wonderful. KC relaxed into the moment, holding Nick's hand like a teenager. They walked and talked, and the day just flew by.

"I'm hungry."

"You ate three muffins."

"That was hours ago."

They found a food trailer with the best pulled pork sandwiches either one had ever tasted. The late lunch filled them up and they continued walking until the sun began to grow lower on the horizon, when they returned to her apartment.

"See you on Monday at the airport." KC reached up on tiptoes and gave Nick a little kiss on the cheek.

"Unless you want to go to church with me tomorrow?"

"Actually, I found a nice little church just a few blocks from my apartment, and I think I will try it tomorrow."

"Good."

"Monday?"

"Monday."

TWENTY

The view when landing in Nevada was different than landing in Seattle. There was no water, and just distant hills. The two-hour flight had been booked enough in advance to allow all three of them to sit together. Ginny promptly turned on her tablet and put on earphones, staying engrossed in a game until they landed. Her seat could have been located out on the wing for all the communication that she offered. Sam and KC sat side-by-side, engrossed in conversation almost the entire flight.

"Did I tell you I have plans to do some remodeling on my house? The kitchen needs some updating, and that shower in the bathroom is just too small."

"Why not just buy a bigger house?"

"No. I moved around so much as a kid, I never want to move again."

"I get that, I do. My parent's house has always been my home base, and I know the comfort in having that."

"Haven't you wanted something of your own?"

"I don't know, maybe. I thought about travel, perhaps working in another country for a while. I've always dreamed about getting a job on a big newspaper in New York or London. Now? I just don't know."

KC sat back in silence for a while, wondering how falling in love with Nick would affect her future. Would she be content to stay where she was? Give up her college dreams? Live in Nick's little house and be happy there?

You are getting way ahead of yourself here, KC. Slow it down.

"Thank goodness we don't have to climb to the lookout tower until tomorrow morning. I want to go play." Ginny made a beeline for the first taxi she saw the minute she had picked up her camera and bag. "Can you take my things with you and leave them with the front desk? I'll see you in the lobby tomorrow at ten."

"Eight," KC and Sam said in unison.

After checking into their hotel rooms, KC and Sam met in the lobby. The flashing lights and loud music were meant to draw them into the casinos as they made their way along the sidewalk, but neither seemed inclined to go inside.

"Just wait until you taste the lunch special."

"I believe you. You have talked about nothing else since we left the hotel. Tell me about Robert. You worked with him, did you say ten years ago?"

"Yeah, we were both pretty much just getting started. He fought fire alongside me a couple of summers. Then about five years ago, we were sent to Nevada to work the fire line."

"And he fell in love with Nevada?"

"Yeah, Nevada and Sophia. Left the fire crew, married Sophia, and opened his own restaurant."

A short time later, KC pushed back her plate and refused a third helping of pasta. The big surprise was not just the incredible food, but the clientele. The RS Grill was the place where all of the firefighters, currently working and retired, hung out. Photos of fires and firefighters were mounted on the walls.

As KC looked at the wall reserved for those who had died, she noticed one young man around Nick's age. For a brief moment, she saw Nick's face in the photo, Nick's eyes smiling into space, on that wall reserved for the fallen. She blinked back tears, and it was once again the picture of a stranger. Her instinct was to turn and run, run away from falling in love with someone she could so easily lose. She remembered a Bible verse that she had memorized many years ago. Psalms 56:3-4 - *What time I am afraid, I will trust in thee.*

Nick came up to her and put his arm around her shoulders. "Are you okay?"

"Yes, I'm just fine." KC smiled, realizing that she really was okay.

She had brought her tablet in her backpack as Nick had suggested, but was not prepared for the amount of information she managed to capture in the few hours they were there.

I owe you big time, Nick.

The afternoon was completed by a nice long walk. Looking at the amazing work that had been put into making Las Vegas a world-renowned vacation spot, she understood why so many people crowded the streets. Fountains of water, bright lights, and surreal architecture could be seen all around them, made more dramatic as the evening came. Yet it was the people themselves that fascinated KC. All nationalities and classes of people were brought together in this one place, and it was quite an experience. Laughter, the universal language, filled the evening.

The next morning found KC and Nick waiting for Ginny in the lobby. Just a few minutes late, she came out of the elevator ready to take on the day.

The drive in the rental car, 150 miles from Las Vegas brought them to the mountain, having climbed to an elevation of 7500 feet. The interview with the fire watcher was really good. He had seen many, many fires in his years as lookout. His sharp memory knew each and every one of them by name and size, and KC did not have the heart to tell him that all of this information could not possibly fit into a human interest column.

Armed with information from that interview and the stories she had amassed from the diner the previous afternoon, KC boarded the airplane that evening tired, but content. The plane had just leveled off when she gave in and laid her head on Nick's shoulder, sleeping the rest of the way home.

The next morning, KC was irritated by the insistent ringing of her phone. She had stayed up late into the night, buoyed by her nap on the plane, and anxious to write her column about Nevada's Ella Mountain Lookout while things were fresh in her mind.

"KC?" Nick's peppy voice was slightly irritating.

"Yeah. Do you know what time it is?"

"I guess the big question is, do you know what time it is?"

KC rubbed her eyes and looked at her clock again. Ten! "Holy Toledo!"

"While we were away playing in Nevada, Ruth came up with some great information for us. Can you pull yourself together for an early lunch? I have a meeting I have to attend later this afternoon."

In an instant, KC was wide awake. "How about that coffee shop near the station?" KC surveyed the clock once again, and mentally added up the time needed to shower, dress, and get there. "Will 11:30 work?"

"Perfect, see you there."

Nick was already waiting, a big grin on his face as KC made her way to the table. As she sat down and crossed her legs, he snickered, but did not comment on her mismatched socks. They both hurriedly ordered the turkey sandwich special, and got quickly to the paperwork that Nick produced from a large envelope.

"Ruth made copies of everything for us. A lot of it was on old microfiche. She said that she would be happy to meet with you and let you look through the information anytime."

"Cool!"

There was a copy of the pay roster from the summer of 1955. Prominently displayed in the list and highlighted with a yellow marker, was the name Jane Johnson.

"Why does her name have four stars next to it?"

"Ruth tells me that she never cashed any of her paychecks, and so there was a special letter in the group of documents with additional information. Wait for it … including an address!"

"No!" The pages were snatched out of his hands as KC leaned into the table to see the information.

"Yes!"

"This address is just outside of Vancouver, Washington. That is less than an hour away."

"And take a look at the name in the paragraph below."

"Mailed to Jane Johnson, care of Kathryn Anderson."

"We found Kathryn!"

"Hold it, Kiddo. We found out where Kathryn lived in 1955. Who knows where she might be now?"

"Okay. I'll calm down. We have to go there and see, at least. Can you get tomorrow off?"

"Already done. I'll pick you up at ten." Nick held up his hand at her protest. "We can leave at eight, fight the morning rush hour traffic, and get there at eleven, or we can leave at ten and get there at eleven."

"You are right." KC gave Nick a resounding kiss right on the lips, right there in the coffee shop.

TWENTY-ONE

The morning could not come fast enough for KC. She was ready and waiting with her tablet and the diary and notebook tucked into her backpack. Nick turned into a little drive-through on the way to the freeway.

"Breakfast sandwich?"

"Yumm!"

"Coffee?"

"Mocha?"

"Done."

Just over an hour later, KC put her phone away as they pulled up in front of a 1930s Cape Cod house, painted a crisp white with abundant flowers growing in tidy beds around it.

"How did people ever find their way before GPS?"

KC punched him in the shoulder. "Beats a map any day."

As they were making their way up the front walk, KC held back. "What if no one is home?"

"Only one way to find out." Nick pulled her along and knocked firmly on the red front door. A little girl opened the door, chocolate smeared on her face and hands and now on the doorknob as well.

"Is your mother home?"

"No."

Okay. "Is there any grown-up home?"

"Gramma, somebody's at the door." With that she disappeared into the back of the house, leaving the door wide open.

"May I help you?" A petite woman with gray hair came to the door. She had a sweet smile and wore an apron splotched with melted chocolate.

"My name is KC Adams. I am a newspaper reporter, and I wondered if I could ask you a few questions?"

Fully expecting to have the door closed in her face, KC instead found herself sitting at a dining room table covered with platters of chocolate chip cookies.

"I know who you are. I've seen your pictures in the Oregon newspaper. Nick, you are so much better looking in person. I am Elizabeth Michaels, but you can call me Beth."

Nick grinned and winked at KC as the woman cleared a spot on the table in front of them, and KC tried her best to ignore him and keep her professional demeanor.

"I'm sorry, there is a big party at Patty's pre-school tomorrow."

"It smells wonderful in here!"

"Would you like a cookie?"

Nick already had two off of the plate before the question was finished.

KC politely declined, and removed the diary from her backpack. In a few short words, she shared the connection between the writer of the diary and Kathryn Anderson.

"As I mentioned, Kathryn was my mother. Mother passed away a few years ago, but I could not give up this wonderful old house, so my son and daughter-in-law and granddaughter moved in with me. May I see the diary?"

Opening it to the first page where Kathryn was mentioned, KC also pulled out the paper with Kathryn's name and address and waited patiently.

"You say that this would have been in 1955? I was just five years old at the time."

"I know it's a long-shot Beth, but do you remember anything that can help?"

Beth thought, munching a cookie as she looked at the diary page again. "Yes! I do remember something. Just before I began first grade that September, my mother had a friend come and stay with us for a while. It may have been just a few days. I remember because she bought me ice cream every afternoon."

Nick quickly swallowed the last bite of his cookie and spoke up "Do you remember her name?"

"My mother called her Dottie."

"Dottie?"

"Yes, I'm pretty sure it was a nick-name, because the lady said it had been a while since she had been called Dottie."

"Beth, do you remember what she looked like?"

"Hmm, not in too much detail. I think she had blonde hair, and I remember that she was shorter than Mom. That's about it. I'm sorry that I could not be any more help."

"You have been great. We have a name, even if it is just a nick-name."

"One more question. Where did your mother go to school?"

"She went to college at the University of Washington. But she went to high school somewhere in northern California. I'll go through her papers in the next few days and call you."

"Thank you, Beth."

"Do you mind signing the newspaper for me? My friends will not believe I met you!"

Beth produced the page with 'On the Lookout' from Sunday's paper, complete with a photo of KC and Nick with their arms around each other looking out over the mountains with the lookout silhouetted behind them.

You have got to be kidding! They ran that photo?

KC was quiet on the way home. Nick knew enough to let her work things out in her head, and did not say a word until they were close to her apartment.

"Earth to KC."

"What? Oh, I'm sorry. I was trying to connect the information we found out today with the list we are making from the diary."

"Oh, so you are not upset about the photo the paper used? I did look awesome!"

KC poked him in the arm. "You always look awesome. I thought *you* would be upset. I have managed to keep your name out of my column, as you requested, until now."

"Yeah, the guys at work will give it to me for sure. If they even read your column."

"Are you saying that *everyone* doesn't read my column? I'm shocked."

Nick pulled up in front of her apartment, but left the car running and did not get out as she gathered her backpack. "See you Saturday?"

"Yes, Saturday. We will definitely finish that diary."

No kiss. No hug.

KC trudged up the stairs and wondered at the inconsistency of falling in love. Shouldn't they be staring deeply into each other's eyes, unable to stay apart? If it *is* real love, should it be this casual?

This love stuff is a complete mystery to me.

Speaking of mysteries, the name of the woman who wrote the diary was definitely not Jane Johnson or Dottie. Tempted as she was to read farther in the diary on her own, KC satisfied her curiosity by re-reading the notes from their little notebook.

"Okay, Notebook, so if we know that there was a ten-acre fire caused by—what did the notes say? *A family with eight children had managed to set their little tent on fire along with the brush and trees around it*. And we know that her daughter would have been six months old the following day. So if we can find out the date of the fire, we can figure out the birth date of the baby. Yes!"

KC placed a call to Nick and asked to meet with Ruth at his office the next day. Nick agreed that this was a good lead, but cautioned her that looking through the archives would be tedious work. As if she had not labored over microfiche and old newspapers in college. This would be a piece of cake.

TWENTY-TWO

The drive to the newspaper office the next morning took longer than walking usually did. She hated the morning traffic, but she needed her car to meet Ruth later that morning. She just had to stop in her office and look at the column set to run on Sunday. She had neglected that last week, and did not want any surprise photos this time.

She set her tea on her desk, along with the maple bar donut she could not resist snatching as she walked past the breakroom, and reviewed the layout for her next column. With Nick's help, she had some great insight from the firefighters in Idaho and had combined her experience in the diner with that of the lookout itself.

***

On the Lookout with KC Adams

September 13

A mere 150 miles from Las Vegas, you enter a completely different world. Gone are the bright lights of the hotels and casinos, replaced by the soft, dappled light of the sun, peaking through the trees and bushes. The voices of so many people speaking at once, the beat of the music, the growl of the traffic, is gone. You hear the sigh of the breeze and the twitter of birds and insects, up here at 7500 feet, where the mountain dances to its own beat.

Of the many lookouts once in existence in Nevada, only three remain active, and this is the only one still manned. Ella Mountain lies in the Clover Mountains, on top of a rocky point. Unlike many of the older lookouts, this one was constructed in 1964 and its two story construction has many modern amenities. However, the purpose stands fast—watch over and protect the land.

The top floor is 15 feet square, enclosed by walls of windows, which provide amazing views in all four directions. The Osborne Fire Finder, a tool in use in fire lookouts since the early 1900s, sits proudly in the center of the room. Also familiar to me were the ever-present binoculars, a wind and temperature gauge, and something not found in the early 1900s, a computer. The telephone there still provides their best means of communication.

Protecting the land is just what the fire lookout, John, has been doing for over 20 years. He has seen many large fires over that time, and I was enthralled as he shared his experiences with me there on the mountain. Nick and I strolled around the building, enjoying the views and the sunshine, absorbing the stories John told, as he pointed to various locations visible from the tower, naming each fire through his two decades as a fire watcher by name.

The past few years have produced a less active fire season, with smaller fires, controlled much more quickly and easily. I have no doubt that this is due largely to the vigilance of this amazing man, the fire lookout, the last of his breed in Nevada.

At a little diner on the outskirts of Las Vegas, I was honored to meet some of the firefighters who have spent their lives protecting Nevada. Many are still working, and travel regularly all over America, wherever fire and smoke put people and their land at risk. It is not an easy job; it is dangerous and challenging at the best of times.

On a small wall next to the counter, a few brave men and women looked down at us from yellowed photos, smiles frozen in time. These were the ones who died fighting the fires that threaten us and our land. Yet not a person in that diner said that they wished they had chosen a different career path. Each one feels called to do this hazardous job, and I, for one, am grateful.

Until next week,

KC Adams

***

The column looked good. Not award winning journalism by any means, but solid. Then CJ looked at the photo Mr. Knitzer had selected. It was an artsy image of Nick and KC holding hands and looking at each other, with the rays of the sun behind them, shining from above the mountains in the distance.

Carol snickered from the other side of the aisle.

"What *is* he thinking?" KC sounded miffed.

"Well, maybe he is thinking this will sell more papers. How long has it been since you have spent any time on social media lately?"

"What?"

"Look!" Carol moved away from her computer screen and ushered KC into her seat.

There was the photo from last Sunday's newspaper, with a cute little caption about lovebirds. KC winced. Carol reached over her shoulder and scrolled down. KC leaned forward with her mouth wide open, but no sound came out. There was another photo of Nick kissing her in front of the restaurant the previous week. Scrolling down more revealed her sleeping on his shoulder aboard the airline flight home. Then there was one of them walking in the park hand in hand.

KC's expression went from incredulous to embarrassment to anger. Words finally came to the surface, but KC managed to control herself before she spoke them out loud. She just kind of gurgled and grabbed her tea cup on the way to the elevator.

Mr. Knitzer's door was open, and KC barged right in. She opened her mouth to complain, but he interrupted her before she could say what was on her mind.

"KC, come in, come in! Your column is generating quite a lot of interest. Good job!"

"Don't you mean the picture of Nick with me is getting the interest?"

"Well, yes, that is true. Frankly, the column from Washington state did not get much of a response at all. Not what I expected. But we'll give the next few a chance and see where it goes. Don't worry."

"I'm not worried. I'm . . ." words failed her.

"Grateful? Happy?" Mr. Knitzer was trying to help but he appeared clueless.

"No. Concerned, surprised, even upset. Are you aware that people have been taking photos of us and posting them online?"

Mr. Knitzer looked puzzled. "Social media interaction with our readers is important in this day and age. It is good for the newspaper."

"This is not about the newspaper, it's about my life. My personal life!"

The thought was dismissed with a wave of his hand. "Next week you and Nick head to northern California, and then to eastern Oregon. Let's see how the next three weeks go with your column. If the interest does not pick up, I will end this current assignment. You do have another story ready?"

"Not quite ready, but almost."

"Good, good. We will talk about it then. Goodbye."

KC found herself standing outside of his office, her protests dismissed as easily as she had been. Well, she and Nick would just have to be careful when they were out in public. Or just stay locked up in her apartment until this was over. Now that was an intriguing idea. KC grinned.

Shut up and get back to work.

The drive to the station to meet with Ruth produced a calming effect. KC put her mind back on the woman who wrote the diary and her child, and off of herself. If Nick was not bothered, she would not be either. After all, the photos on the computer were quickly forgotten and replaced with new and more exciting posts. The story of the diary, however, would not be so easily forgotten. If she could find out the identity of this mysterious woman and find her child, then reunite them, and cover the entire process in her column, this could be a great story. It just might be the best story ever!

KC parked her car and grabbed her backpack, then made her way to the front office. As she walked through the front door, memories of meeting Nick for the first time caused her to smile. Who knew that day would change her life forever? A quick call to Nick from the woman at the front desk, a short walk up the stairs, and she found herself at his desk, doing her best not to hug him and to stop grinning like a crazy woman.

Luckily for Nick, the rest of the office was mostly empty. He walked her to the back of the room, where a woman was on her knees, going through the drawers of a little rolling file cabinet and pulling out microfiche cards.

Ruth Campos stood up, surprisingly tall and agile. Her bright red hair and big brown eyes lined with electric blue eyeliner matched her colorful sweater and bright enthusiasm as she bypassed the usual handshake and gave KC a big hug. "KC! I feel like I know you already. Nick has said such nice things about you. I got your message about the fire from 1955 and I have something exciting to show you both."

Nick and KC leaned in toward the microfiche reader as Ruth expertly moved the page around until she found just what she was looking for in the middle of the page.

Nick read it out loud. "Ten-acre fire took place on June 23, 1955 near the Eagle Butte campground. Cause, tent fire. Fire name: Tent Fire."

"That's it!"

"Whoa, hold on there. It may be the fire she referred to, but we can't be sure."

Ruth stood up and led them to a table at the back of the room. "KC, these are the newspaper clippings from 1950 – 1959. You might find corroborating evidence in there. Make yourself comfortable, and I will check in with you in a few hours. I have an appointment with a doctor."

"Are you okay?" Nick sounded concerned.

Ruth's brown eyes twinkled. "I'm just fine. I have an early lunch date with a doctor. I'll let you know how it goes and if he is a contender as a companion for the cruise I have planned to the Bahamas this winter."

Nick reluctantly returned to his desk, and KC nestled into the padded chair at the old table, surrounded by boxes of old newspapers and photos.

I wish your picture would magically appear, Mystery Woman. Well, wishing will get me nowhere.

Buoyed by the information on the film and determined to find even more, KC called on her previous research experience and began to go through the old newspapers. She was more than halfway through the pile by the time Ruth returned.

"These stories from the 1950s are fascinating, and I have to keep reminding myself to stick with finding out about the fire."

"Yeah? Well, I lived through the 1950s and they were nothing special."

"Bad lunch date?"

"I can cross the doctor off of the list. Talked about himself the entire time, and a napkin appears to be a foreign object to him."

"Eww!"

"Yeah."

Ruth contented herself with bringing order to the chaos of the boxes, and KC continued her search.

"Got it!"

Nick was at the back of the room in seconds.

***

June 23, 1955. The Benton's, a family from nearby Jenson Creek, was camping in the Huckleberry Campground when a candle accidentally set fire to their tent. None of the eight children were injured, and the fire was spotted from the Iliana Lookout Tower and reported quickly. The local fire crew responded immediately, and the Tent Fire was contained at just under ten acres. The family beagle, Ducky, is still missing. If you find him, please call ...

***

KC could barely contain her excitement. "Do you know what this means?"

Nick grinned. "We have a birthdate!"

"Yes! Christmas Eve, 1954."

TWENTY-THREE

KC woke up early on Saturday, the contents of the rest of the diary just a few hours away from revealing their secrets. She tugged on a hoodie and some fuzzy socks and headed into the kitchen to make a cup of tea. As she passed the diary, which was laying enticingly on the coffee table in front of the couch, she sighed loudly. Grabbing a bowl of left-over popcorn, KC took one bite, and threw the rest in the trashcan. Tea in hand, she headed toward her bedroom, again passing by the diary which taunted her, sitting there determinedly closed.

I wish I hadn't made that stupid pact with Nick to read through this together. No, I'm glad I did. I think. I need a hot shower.

Showered, dressed, and ready to get started, KC made a pot of coffee. It was Nick's turn to bring breakfast, or she would have filled the time baking something. She needed something sweet. As if reading her mind, Nick arrived a half-hour early with an unusual breakfast assortment of cheeses, fruit and donuts.

"Quick review?"

"Good idea. Jane Johnson, not her real name, nickname Dottie. Short, blonde, green eyes. Gave baby girl up for adoption, father of child deceased. Rich family, father a senator, mother deceased, younger sister. Purple dragon, nanny named Margie. Year, 1955. Nick grabbed a pen and added to the list. Baby born Dec 24, 1954."

"Good, let's get to the rest of the diary."

"Are you sure you've had enough breakfast? We can wait if you want some more."

KC punched him in the arm and opened the diary.

***

I had a vivid dream last night, waking early this morning. It is so clear in my thoughts, almost like a memory. I was walking through Capitol Park, enjoying the flowers and the different varieties of trees, when a young girl came flying past me on a bicycle where Thirteenth Street crosses the park. She had red braids and big, blue eyes, and I knew in an instant that this was my Sara. I reached out to her, but woke up suddenly. Perhaps I will see her someday. Will I know her when I do?

***

Nick was writing the information in the notebook before KC could even make a comment. "Now those are some tangible clues."

"I'll get my tablet."

KC typed in 'Capitol Park' in the search engine.

"Oh, that's just great! Seattle, Salem, Atlanta, Detroit, DC. Does every state have a Capitol Park?"

"Looks that way. Try adding in Thirteenth Street."

"Okay. That is better. Most hits point to Sacramento."

Just then KC's phone rang, and KC closed the diary and took it with her to the kitchen to make sure that Nick would not read ahead without her.

She returned with her phone on speaker. "It's Elizabeth Michaels, Kathryn's daughter."

"Ah, the best chocolate chip cookie maker in the world."

Beth giggled in the background. "Well, I told you that I would look through Mom's old papers and let you know where she went to high school."

KC heard rustling papers as Beth paused. "Did you find anything?" KC asked impatiently.

"Oh, yes, yes I did. I could not find her yearbooks, but I did find her high school diploma. She graduated in June 1954, from Sacramento High School, in Sacramento, California."

Nick practically jumped off the couch when KC shouted "Dragon!"

"Dragon?"

"Yes, purple dragon."

Beth spoke up. "Is everything okay there?"

"Oh yes, everything is wonderful. Thank you so much for your help! I'll let you know how the search goes."

KC picked up her tablet again and searched for high school, Sacramento, California. There were several choices, and she clicked on Sacramento High Charter School. There was a comment on the right of her screen. "Love my HS dragons!" Further research showed that Sacramento High School closed in 2003 and reopened as a charter school. They kept the same mascot, a dragon, and the school colors, purple and white.

"Purple dragon!" they shouted in unison.

Excited to continue uncovering clues, they turned the pages of the diary. Nothing. Lists of chores. Pretty poetry about the mountains and trees.

***

High it reaches to the sky, the mountain, large and stout

We join you as you reach toward God, the sturdy trees call out

With branches pointing up they grow, determined to grow tall

When one small bird flies toward the clouds

Much higher than them all

***

"Nice, but not very helpful. Here is something, on the last written page. The rest are blank."

***

I have matured over the course of this summer, but I hold no delusions that I will be able to hold my own with Father. I leave here soon, and will spend my last week of freedom with Kathryn. My sister will meet me there and we will return home together as if just returning from Europe. My newfound faith makes me cringe at this deception. Yet I am not willing to pay the consequences for my disobedience to Father.

Oh, dear, the young men who are coming to carry my belongings down the mountain are here early. I will tuck this diary into the little hiding place, and try to retrieve it just before we leave.

***

"Well, apparently she never had the opportunity to go back and get the diary."

"Or perhaps she just forgot about it."

"Still, we have a few more clues. She mentioned Kathryn again. If her father was well-known, perhaps we can find some mention of the sister's trip to Europe in the newspaper archives from Sacramento."

"Which would mean that we would actually have to go to Sacramento."

Oh, yeah.

Nick put his arm around KC's shoulders and hugged her. What was meant as a gesture of comfort, led to a small little kiss, then to a longer kiss. Then the phone rang again.

Really?

"KC, it's Ginny. I picked up your plane tickets at the office. You forgot them on Friday. Meet you at the airport at eight on Monday?"

"Oh, yes, Monday. I totally forgot! Where are we going, anyway?"

"Banner Mountain Lookout Tower, near Nevada City. We fly into Sacramento. It's about an hour and a half drive from there."

"Sacramento?"

"Yes."

"Sacramento!" KC and Nick shouted in unison. Ginny muttered something about crazy reporters and hung up.

TWENTY-FOUR

The plane landed at the Sacramento airport shortly after take-off from Portland. KC sat near the window with Ginny in the middle and Nick on the aisle. She was becoming paranoid about people taking photos and posting them for all to see. Nick thought it was funny, but since he was getting a lot of flak at work about it, he humored her paranoia.

"I'll get the rental car and you two can wait for the luggage."

"Impatient men!" KC commented under her breath as she stood by the conveyor belt, tapping her foot.

Ginny wisely kept her mouth shut.

They stopped very briefly at the hotel, just long enough to check in and drop off their bags. Grabbing a quick lunch on the way, they headed out to the lookout tower.

As the car wove in and out of Sacramento traffic, KC's impatience seemed to grow.

"Thinking about your other story?"

"Yes, I want to do this one justice, but my heart is not in it."

Ginny spoke up from the back seat. "You two have another story? Do you need a good photographer?"

"I'm working on a story. No photographs needed yet, but I'll be sure to let you know."

Nick put his arm around KC's shoulders, and Ginny snapped a picture.

Give me a break!

The terrain changed from city to country in a short amount of time, and as they headed toward the mountains, KC found her tension fading.

She remembered a Bible verse she had memorized when she was a teen. *Psalm 96:11-12 Let the heavens rejoice, let the earth be glad; let the sea resound, and all that is in it. Let the fields be jubilant, and everything in them; let all the trees of the forest sing for joy.* The trees around her were definitely singing for joy as the sun beat down on them on this beautiful day. KC sighed in contentment.

They arrived at the impressive tower by mid-afternoon. The sun was high in the sky, a bright white light against cloudless blue. Nick and KC climbed the 60 feet up the stairs, while Ginny put the magic of her camera to work in a series of shots looking up toward the top.

The woman who was working that afternoon was pleasant and knowledgeable, and KC took some good notes on the history of the tower. Built of wood in 1911, it had been rebuilt out of steel in 1926, and renovated in 1948. It had been manned by the first women's liberation fire lookout crew in the early 1970s. She made notes of the updates to the structure over the years and the current schedule of people who manned it now. Banner Lookout tower was different than the others they had visited. Its top, created for easy viewing, did not contain living facilities. Fire watchers worked in four hour shifts during the fire season. Nick and KC politely listened to a few stories about forest fires, the information not much different than those they had heard in Washington and Nevada.

Boring. If I'm bored, even looking out over this magnificent view, my readers will be too.

As Nick and KC walked down the steps, KC realized that this time there would be no redemption for this series of stories. Not even if they printed the photo of Nick kissing her at the top. If she could not find the information she needed to solve the mystery of the red diary, she had no idea where her column would go next, if it went anywhere at all.

On the drive back to the hotel, Ginny climbed into her usual backseat position and promptly fell asleep.

"Nick, what would you think of staying in Sacramento for a few extra days and doing some research?"

"I think it is an excellent idea. I have a few days of leave I can take before my team is up again."

To go back out on the fire line, back into danger. Get your act together, KC. Focus on the story.

"I'll get the tickets changed to Thursday as soon as we get back."

"We're not going back until Thursday?" Ginny leaned forward and yawned.

"*You* are going back in the morning. KC and I are staying a few extra days."

"Without me?"

"Without you."

The following morning, Nick drove Ginny to the airport and KC spent a few hours doing research on her tablet. Her big break came when she went down to the front desk to see if they had any maps of the area.

"Hey, do you happen to know anyone who might know if the Sacramento Charter High School has any of the old yearbooks from the 1950s?"

"My Aunt Denise is a teacher there. She is an expert on the history of the school, and the president of the Alumni Association. I can text her if you like. She usually responds to me fairly quickly."

KC returned to her room with a map of the city and a huge new lead. The Central branch of the Sacramento Public Library had all of the old yearbooks. She waited like a kid on Christmas morning for Nick to return from the airport.

The walk to the library was pleasant, the people they passed chatting happily with each other, the day was warm and sunny. KC looked at every face, wondering as they walked around each corner if she would by chance see their mystery woman.

"Don't I get some lunch before we bury ourselves in the archives of the library?"

"You just ate breakfast a few hours ago."

"Hey, they have burritos!"

THE STORY OF THE YEAR

After a quick but satisfying lunch, Nick walked with an impatient KC toward the huge glass doors of the library. An impressive building from the outside, they were awed by the size of the library they found on the inside. The Central Branch had high ceilings with arched windows casting light on the full bookshelves below. Tables and chairs offered a place to read or study. KC claimed one for herself and unloaded her tablet from her backpack.

"If I lived nearby, I would spend hours in this place. It is fabulous!"

"Shhh!"

"Hush yourself. Are you ready to get started?"

"It will take us hours just to find what we are looking for."

"Or—we could ask for directions."

"Or we could ask for directions."

Men!

A tall, thin man with graying hair and a serious expression stood behind the reference counter. He was able to direct them to the section containing the yearbooks from the old Sacramento High School. The school was founded in 1856, and although they did not have actual yearbooks from that long ago, there were still rows and rows of them.

"Are they in order?"

"Umm, mostly in order."

KC skimmed through the shelves with a practiced eye, her years of journalism studies from college requiring a lot of time in libraries. Yes, there was a lot of information on the Internet, and it was often much easier to search from the comfort of your own dorm room. Her professors had encouraged her, however, to love working with the printed page. She still preferred to read her books by turning actual pages, rather than the more popular digital versions.

"1950, 1951, 1952, 1953, 1955 . . . No!"

"Okay, let's look on either side. I'll work forward in time, and you go backward."

A full half-hour had elapsed and neither of them had found the yearbook they were seeking. Nick gave up and joined KC as she continued to search, and stole a quick kiss just as the man from the reference desk came around the corner.

Busted!

KC looked at the man, who was blushing, and saw that he was carrying a yearbook under his arm.

"Excuse me, Miss. I was sorting books for restacking, and I noticed this yearbook from 1954."

KC snatched it out of his hand with an effusive, "Thank you, thank you!"

Nick grinned "I was pretty sure that you were about to kiss him if he had not backed away so quickly."

"Well, you never know."

Back at their little table, KC and Nick sat side-by-side, the coveted yearbook in front of them.

Skimming past the photos of the faculty and the football team, KC paused at the montage of photos with captions from the graduating class. *Most likely to succeed in show business* revealed two young girls in stage makeup. *Most likely to end up in jail* was posted above a photo of three boys wearing identical white T-shirts and sporting well-combed hairstyles. Looking at each photo carefully, KC turned the page with a sigh. *Most likely to marry royalty* caught her attention. Two young women smiled regally for the camera, one wearing a polka-dot dress. Kathryn Williams and Caroline 'Dottie' Smith.

KC nearly fell off of her chair in her excitement.

"That's it! That is a photo of our mystery woman, Caroline Smith."

"Hey, Ms. Journalist, slow down. That is *probably* a photo of our mystery woman."

"Yeah, yeah. I know." KC turned the pages to the individual photos, and found the one for Caroline Smith. Though the photos were black-and-white, she was clearly a blond, and was wearing a polka-dot blouse.

Nick reached over and flipped a few more pages until he came to the group photos. Glee club, science club, debate club. And there was Caroline Smith in the photo and on the list for the debate club.

"Do you remember that she said she joined the debate club to please her father?"

"You are a genius. I do remember, now that you mention it. Jane Johnson *must* be Caroline Smith!"

"The clues are certainly stacking up. I want to search the old newspaper archives while I'm here to see if there is any mention of her. If her father was a rich senator, there should be something."

"It's almost dinner time, can we come back in the morning?"

"Just let me photocopy these pages."

KC was about to joke with Nick about his obsession with food, when her own stomach gave a loud and un-ladylike rumble.

"First thing in the morning."

"I promise."

A knock on her door woke KC from a sound sleep just before daylight the following morning. KC slipped her hoodie over her pajamas and looked through the peep hole in the door to see Nick standing there, fully dressed.

"Nick? When I said 'first thing in the morning' I did not mean ..." KC looked over at the clock on her nightstand. "... a quarter to six."

"I know, and I'm sorry to wake you, but there is a fire just south of here and my team has been called. I'm taking off in just a few minutes."

KC felt that instantaneous fear tighten her chest, and took a deep breath before speaking. She managed to get the words out, hoping the waver in her voice sounded like she had just woken up, and not like she was in an inward state of panic. "Okay, just be safe out there."

"I'll be fine. If you find Caroline Smith, will you wait to speak with her until I get back? I'd hate to miss out on that."

"Sure. Leave me with all of the tedious research, then step in for the glory moment."

"I will personally drive you back to Sacramento or wherever we end up."

"That's a deal. Now get going."

Nick leaned in for a quick kiss on the cheek and left. KC closed the door and leaned back against it.

Get going before you see me cry.

Making her way back to the bed, KC wiped her eyes with the back of her hand, reached into the drawer of her nightstand, and pulled out the Bible. She searched frantically for some words of encouragement, something that would calm her. She knew just the verse that she was looking for, but her fumbling fingers had a hard time finding it. *2 Timothy 1:7 - For God hath not given us the spirit of fear; but of power, and of love, and of a sound mind.* KC read the verse again, then put away the Bible and headed into the bathroom for a hot shower.

"Lord, help me to trust you. Please keep Nick safe." She repeated the prayer several times as the steamy water and God's promise poured over her until she felt totally calm.

After a large breakfast at the hotel coffee shop, and a sufficient amount of caffeine, KC tossed a few protein bars into her backpack along with a bottle of water, and headed for the library. She was waiting when they unlocked the front door. She chose the same table and chair that she and Nick had sat at the previous day, unloaded her backpack, and headed for the reference desk. The nice man from the day before was not there, but a sweet young woman gladly directed her to the old microfiche drawers and readers.

Immersed in reading the articles from the old newspapers, KC worked diligently. A group of teenagers sauntered past her, laughing and teasing each other as they went by.

What are these kids doing out of school? Oh, my goodness, it's nearly four!

KC stood up and stretched her tight back. She had been bent over those old slides all day long, with only a few small breaks. She had an impressive amount of information, and could not wait to type it up into a coherent set of notes. An Internet search would likely reveal even more than she could glean from the old newspapers, but what she had already compiled was more than she had ever anticipated.

TWENTY-FIVE

Friday morning brought some unexpected rain. Perhaps the fire that Nick had been dispatched to would be helped by the change in the weather. Unfortunately, the rain lasted just a few hours and never made it south, across the California line.

KC had finished her lack-luster column on Banner Mountain Lookout Tower, doing her best to make it as interesting as possible for her readers. Mr. Knitzer selected a photo of Nick kissing her at the top of the stairs, which came as no surprise to KC. The social media pages were replete with comments on the two of them, but not much was mentioned about the actual content of the column itself.

Nick managed to call from the fire camp on Sunday afternoon.

"I'm just checking in to let you know that I'm okay."

"I appreciate that, but you know that you don't need to check in with me."

"Maybe I just miss hearing your voice."

"Well, that's different. I miss you too."

More than you know.

He did not ask about her research into Caroline Smith, and she did not offer up any information. It would wait until he was home.

Monday, she was scheduled to head to Eastern Oregon and visit one last lookout tower. Ginny had another assignment, which left KC totally on her own. The trip took her close to her parent's house, and so she headed there after she finished her interview.

After a day of resting and being pampered, she spent the next day compiling the information she had collected at the Sacramento Library. Nick did not call, but KC really did not expect him to. The following day, KC tackled her newspaper column.

Seated at her father's desk in the little office, KC wrote the last of the fire lookout columns. She was both sad to put an ending to what had started as such an unexpected adventure, and happy to finally be done with the travel and repetitive subject matter.

***

On the Lookout with KC Adams

September 27

I am happy to share with you my visit to the final lookout tower on our fascinating summer of exploration into the world of the fire watchers. In our own Oregon mountains hides the classic lookout of Mt. Pisgah, first established in 1918.

As with many of the others, it has undergone a series of renovations over time, and is a fully functioning and comfortable home to the man who has watched over our land for many years. Overlooking the north side of Big Summit Prairie, this amazing structure in the Ochoco Mountains has covered many forest fires over decades of dedicated service. While others have fallen into decay, or been relegated to the task of a glorified campsite, Mt. Pisgah remains an integral part of detecting fires.

In the clear, bright afternoon sunshine, I was able to spot several other lookout towers using a powerful scope, several of them abandoned shells of their former selves. I could imagine watching lightning streak across the sky, or seeing the smoke from a fire and calling in the location.

Many lookouts are being replaced by technical gadgets and computers, yet this tower is assured of being here for many years to come. There is nothing as reliable as someone with a good pair of binoculars and an impressively strong spotting scope, along with the sincere dedication to protect our lands.

As I drove carefully down the winding road, I felt a little sadness at the end of this summer adventure. And yet I write this column with a big smile on my face as I share with all of you a secret.

Next week I begin the most intriguing, heartrending, soul-satisfying series of columns that I have ever written. I look forward to taking you with me on a journey that crosses decades of time and solves a mystery that sat surrounded by dust, high in the mountains, hidden in the Iliana Lookout Tower for many years.

Until next week,

KC Adams

***

KC uploaded the final column on lookout towers, along with a so-so photo of the tower itself that she had snapped from her phone. No one would care about the photo anyway, since Nick was not in it. They probably would not care about the column, either.

"KC, would you like some fresh-baked snickerdoodle cookies?"

I love working from home!

"Sure, Mom. Do you have any iced tea?"

The keys on the computer clicked away tirelessly as afternoon became evening. KC lost all track of time, surprised when her father pulled her away from the little office for dinner.

"Dad, this research is fantastic. I thought this was going to be just a nice story, but once I started digging into it, I can see that this is big. I mean really, really big. It could be the best story I have ever written!"

"Do you want to talk about it?"

"No!"

"Okay, okay! Do you want to pass the potatoes?"

When dinner was over, KC headed right back into the office to continue her research.

THE STORY OF THE YEAR

Midnight came with the unexpected sound of her phone beeping the presence of a text message. KC had been so busy compiling her research into a readable format that she had not noticed how quiet and dark the house had become.

She read the text out loud "Home safe and sound. Call you tomorrow. Love, Nick."

Love, Nick.

"Thank you, Lord."

With a final few clicks, KC finished the last of her work, printed everything off and put it away in her backpack, then headed to bed.

TWENTY-SIX

Saturday morning brought with it some clouds and a few rain drops. It was the last Saturday of September, and autumn was beginning to settle in. KC was up early, preparing a frittata for breakfast for Nick when he arrived. She put on a pot of coffee and made sure that the diary, the little notebook, the photocopies from the library, and all of her meticulously typed notes were laid out in order on the coffee table.

Nick had called late the previous morning, still sounding tired from his fire duty in California.

"Wow, what a brutal week! It was a lot of work, with long hours, but my crew did great. How was your week?"

"I can hardly wait to show you all of the information I found. But I know you are tired. It will wait until Saturday."

"Really? That's it? Not even a hint?"

"Nope. Let's wait until we are together."

"Yeah, my brain and body are both too tired to appreciate it now, let alone remember anything you tell me."

What if I told you I loved you? Would you remember that?

They agreed to hold off discussing KC's research until they could do so in person. KC had barely slept, so anxious to share what she had found.

The doorbell rang.

It's Nick!

KC pulled open the door so quickly he almost fell over, and then planted a big kiss right on his surprised lips. He returned the kiss with gusto, holding KC up in his strong arms as she nearly fell over.

Breakfast seemed slow, the impatient tapping of her foot against the floor evidence of her impatience. "Okay, KC, I get the hint. But this was really delicious. Now, let's see what has you so excited."

"Be prepared for a big surprise."

"Bigger than a kiss on your doorstep and a frittata?"

KC punched Nick in the arm as they settled into their familiar positions on the little couch.

"Were you able to confirm that Caroline Smith is our mystery woman?"

"Oh yes, that and a lot more. Here are some copies of the newspaper stories I found at the library. I highlighted the important parts."

***

Caroline and Dorothy Smith, daughters of Senator William Smith, were seen playing on the White House lawn with President Truman's dog, a cocker spaniel named Feller. The first term Senator was in Washington to meet with the President on matters pertaining to his economic oversight committee.

***

Caroline Smith places first in the semi-finals of the Sacramento High Debate Team.

***

Caroline and Dorothy Smith host the Senator's annual Fourth of July Party. No expense is spared for this highlight of the social season in Hanson Heights.

***

Caroline Smith graduates with honors. Valedictorian for the Sacramento High class of '54.

***

June 1, 1955: Miss Caroline Smith and her sister, Dorothy, are planning an extended vacation in Europe this summer.

***

"Well, that is pretty good proof right there. That lines up perfectly with what we found in the diary. Did they mention the nanny?"

"No, they did not mention the nanny. The information from the old newspapers was enough to satisfy me. Caroline Smith did write that diary. That, however, is not the most exciting part of my research."

KC produced the pages that she had printed out in her father's office. "Caroline Smith is *the* Carol Smith of Smith and Johnson Industries."

"Carol Smith? Like, one of the richest and most influential women in America?"

"Yep."

"Wow!"

"My research showed that the Smiths hit it big in the gold mines of the Sacramento area some generations back. Unlike many of the men who squandered their sudden wealth, Caroline's great-grandfather invested wisely and passed on that fortune through the generations. Her father started his business venture right out of college, with his roommate as a partner. Later, he was a two-term senator, and then returned to his company, bought out his partner, and grew Smith and Johnson Industries into a billion-dollar corporation."

"I'll bet Johnson wished he had kept his half!"

"Oh, yes. He even tried to sue Senator Smith, but he did not have a case. It was all on the up-and-up. Johnson died shortly after that."

KC picked up their coffee cups and headed into the kitchen to refill them. She turned around and found Nick right behind her. Close enough to kiss. And so they did. Followed by a nice, long hug and one more kiss.

"Back to work!" KC was nearly breathless.

Seated in his usual place on the couch, Nick leaned back and KC continued.

"So, Caroline attended the University of Washington with her friend, Kathryn, and graduated with a degree in business in 1959. Her sister, Dorothy, died in a boating accident when she was just twenty. Caroline worked for her father, but not much more was written about her until he died unexpectedly in 1984. When she took over the company, it was doing okay, but she modernized everything and went international, and turned it into an even bigger success."

"Did she have more children?"

"No, she never married, never had a family. The research indicates that she put all of her time and effort into the company. Except for a few photos of her at charity events, there is no mention of any social interactions or anything really personal at all. She is a very private woman."

"I seem to remember reading that she traveled to Japan recently to close some business deal, as part of a multi-country business trip. It stands out in my mind, because I was thinking as I read it that I hope I have that much energy when I am eighty."

KC put her notes down on the table, and laid the diary on top. Leaning forward with her elbows on her knees, she stared at the diary. "It is hard for me to reconcile the tender-hearted woman from the diary with the hard business woman I read about."

"Well, it has been over sixty years."

"Yes, but it is sad that she never fell in love again, or had a chance to have another baby."

"Speaking of baby, what is your plan for finding her daughter?"

"I have a meeting scheduled with an adoption lawyer on Tuesday. I'll find out what options we have and let you know. I was thinking, even if we don't find the daughter, just the fact that Carol Smith had an illegitimate child is big news."

"For a tabloid, perhaps. You are not thinking of writing about that?"

"No, no, of course not. But it would be quite a story, wouldn't it?"

"KC, this is a woman's private life you're playing with here. Don't you remember her pain as she wrote in the diary?"

"Nick, don't worry. I'll do some research on babies born in Sacramento on December 24, 1955 and let you know what I find. My goal is still to reunite the mother and daughter."

KC walked Nick to the door and they shared one final kiss before he headed home. Her mind was on her next step—finding Caroline's daughter.

***

Monday morning came, and the first heavy fall rain came with it. KC put away her strappy sandals and pulled her boots down from the top shelf of her closet. She dusted off her umbrella and headed out for her walk to the office.

Feeling a chill, she stopped in to her local coffee place, and ordered a large hot cocoa. Behind her in line, a young girl was begging for a pastry. "Please, Aunt Alice, that scone looks so good! I'll share it with you."

Bingo!

KC grabbed her cup of cocoa and practically jogged the two blocks to her office, trying not to spill any. She turned on her computer and waited for the screen to come up, tapping her foot impatiently. In the diary, Caroline had said that she went to stay with her aunt when she was pregnant. She was going to look for children born in Sacramento, but what if she had the child while staying with her aunt? Thank goodness for genealogy sites. Caroline Smith had two aunts, both on her mother's side. One lived in Tucson, Arizona and one right there in Portland.

Amanda peeked over the divider, startling KC as she was writing down the information. "What are you doing here?"

"Working."

"You are supposed to be in the meeting upstairs. Didn't you see the note from Darlene on your desk or read your emails?"

"No and no. I'm going now!" KC chugged down the last of her cocoa and wiped her mouth with the back of her hand, then grabbed her notepad and pen, and made a dash to the elevator.

THE STORY OF THE YEAR

The meeting was well underway when KC tried to slip in quietly, sliding silently into a chair at the back of the table. No one seemed to notice, and she breathed a sigh of relief. It was a short-lived reprieve. When Mr. Knitzer finished with the political story he was assigning, he turned to her.

"KC, good to see you. As we have discussed previously, these stories about the fire lookout towers have run their course. Traveling to other lookouts just did not capture the attention of our readers. You told me that you're working on another story. Well, let's hear it. It had better be a good one, because the *On the Lookout* column is in serious jeopardy right now."

KC had to bite her tongue to keep from mentioning that traveling to other lookouts was the editor's idea, or rather, his wife's idea. She took a deep breath and launched into her pitch for the next story.

"I don't know if you remember, but in one of my earlier columns from Iliana I mentioned finding an old, red, diary hidden beneath the bed."

The sports columnist spoke up, "I remember that one—you were being attacked by a vicious bat at the time. Right?"

"Yes, that is correct." KC managed to smile. "Well, after a great deal of research, I have found that the diary was written in 1955. It outlines the life and love of a young woman who was a fire watcher for just one summer, including the death of the man she loved, and the birth of a daughter, whom she gave up for adoption."

"Are you sure that you found a diary and not an old romance novel?"

The political writer was silenced by a single look from Mr. Knitzer. "Go on."

"I intend to find the daughter and reunite her with the mother."

"I take it you have already found the mother?"

"Yes, I've identified the mother."

"Interesting, but not necessarily something that would sell papers."

"I have a lot of research left to do, but I plan to orchestrate the reunion to happen just before Christmas, and document each step in my weekly column. The baby that was given up for adoption was born on Christmas Eve."

"Nice!" the political writer said.

"Yes, nice. Perhaps enough, but I'm not totally sold yet. Give me something else here."

KC took a big breath, ignored her conscience, which was warning her not to do it, and blurted out, "The mother is a very, very high profile woman."

"Name?"

"Not gonna happen here, sorry."

"No, no, you are absolutely right. Keep the readers guessing until the last minute. Excellent, excellent. The story is yours. Go with it. If it turns out as you say, it just might be the story of the year."

TWENTY-SEVEN

By Tuesday morning, the rain had turned into a downpour. KC had a meeting to interview an adoption attorney later that morning, and a lunch date with Nick. She spent a little extra time with her makeup and choosing an outfit as she got ready.

I don't care what the lawyer thinks, but I want Nick to see me at my best.

KC looked at the clock.

Late again!

She grabbed her backpack, shoved in the notebook along with all of her notes and print-outs, made sure her tablet was there, and headed out to her car.

Mr. Magellan was a nice, middle-aged man with short, blond hair. A photo of his wife and five blond children lined up by age and size sat prominently on his desk.

"Ms. Adams, I understand that you are a reporter, and here to ask general questions about adoption?"

"That's correct. And please, call me KC."

"Okay, KC, feel free to ask. But I hope you understand that I will not divulge any specific information or names of my clients."

"Of course. I am really looking for information on a child who was put up for adoption many years ago."

"How many years ago?"

"In 1954."

"Oh dear, that is a real problem. In that generation, those cases were generally handled as closed adoptions. No information was available to either the birth parents or the child. It was thought best for all involved that the information be kept confidential. For years now, there have been open adoptions, with the current thinking that for psychological and health reasons, the specifics should be made available to the parties involved."

"So you are telling me that even if I can find the law firm that handled the adoption, they would not be able to share any information?"

"That's correct."

"Do you have any advice for me, then?"

"Actually, I do. Look on the Internet. There are a lot of sites where adopted children, birth parents, and even siblings, can post information seeking to find their biological family. Just be careful not to fall into the trap of those websites where they ask you to pay to find the names. There are a lot of charlatan's online, I'm afraid."

"I'll be careful, then. Thank you so much for your time and your advice. Would it be okay if I use your name in my column?"

"Certainly, here is my card. Just be kind."

"Absolutely! You have been very generous with your time. Thank you again." KC put her tablet into her backpack and let herself out of the office.

It was just a quarter past eleven when KC arrived at the restaurant. Nick was not due to arrive for another forty-five minutes. KC ordered some hot tea and pulled out her notebook. She jotted down a few paragraphs of a column, just trying out the words, seeing how well they flowed. The meeting at the newspaper office the previous day was still on her mind. A little voice reprimanded her for mentioning the fact that the mother was a high-profile woman.

Give it a rest—I didn't give them her name.

KC ignored the automatic twinge of her conscience. Was she even considering doing that? What if Mr. Knitzer demanded to know? Would she be willing to compromise her ethics, to share a secret kept closely all of these years, to embarrass Caroline Smith and perhaps her daughter, just to get ratings? Just to keep her job at the paper? A job that she had worked hard to achieve.

Get tough, KC. You are a reporter, after all.

Just as her conscience was about the step in and challenge her thinking, Nick arrived.

They each ordered the hot roast beef sandwich special, and then leaned in across the table toward each other, sharing the events of the day. They talked about the weather, the latest news story, memories from their pasts. Conversation with Nick was so easy. They held hands under the table, something they had started when the photos of them together out in public began appearing on social media. At the arrival of their lunch, they broke contact, and KC's hand felt suddenly cold. Nick grinned at her, as if he understood what she was feeling.

Was this what love felt like? Needing to be together all of the time. Feeling sad and empty when you were alone. Had she felt like this when she was in college and so deeply in love with . . . oh dear! What was his name? Derrick. His name was Derrick. How could she have forgotten, even for a moment? Were her feelings for him just youthful infatuation?

I was ready to marry him! How could I have come so close to making such a huge mistake? I still miss Derrick, don't I? Do I?

A lone tear made its way down her cheek, and she quickly wiped it off and excused herself to go to the restroom, hoping that Nick had not noticed.

In her rush to leave the table, KC's sleeve caught on the edge of her backpack, sending it flying to the floor. She did not pause to pick it up as she walked swiftly around the counter and down the hall. Nick looked a little perplexed at her quick departure, but he just shrugged it off and bent down to retrieve the contents of her backpack. Once the tablet and printouts were in place, he picked up the notebook and straightened the bent pages. There it was, in pen and ink, in KC's handwriting.

***

On the Lookout with KC Adams

As I unveiled the mystery of the old, red, diary that I found at Iliana, I was drawn to the plight of the young woman who wrote it. She poured out her heart, crying for the man who died, and the child that she gave up for adoption. What

> *kind of a woman was she, this young mother? As I searched for her identity, I never expected to find out that this poetic young woman, the bereaved girlfriend of a secret lover, was none other than Carol Smith, of Smith and Johnson Industries. I am excited to share with you that I have uncovered this secret that she has kept for more than sixty years.*

***

Nick was sitting there with a shocked look on his face, the notebook still in his hand, when KC came back to the table.

She looked down at the page on the notebook that he held. "Nick, it's not what you think."

"Really? It seems pretty clear to me."

"I was just jotting down some words while I was waiting for you to arrive. I have no intention of actually using that." She reached out and snatched to notebook and stuffed it into her backpack, as if trying to take back the words Nick had read.

"KC, if you did not plan to use it, you would never have written it. Sometimes your words reveal what is in your heart, even when you least expect it."

"No! I promised not to use her name, and I am going to hold to that promise."

"I hope that's true. I'm going to pray that God will guide you when you write, and that your motive for reuniting this woman and her child is not just to sell papers or become famous."

Nick stood up, tossed some money on the table, kissed KC on the cheek, and left her standing alone.

"Are we still on to go to my parents on Saturday morning?" KC called to Nick's retreating back, but he did not turn around or respond.

Several days passed, and KC kept her phone turned on and with her at all times, just in case Nick called. Nothing. She tried calling him, but got his voicemail. She left a couple of messages, then decided it was futile to call again. It was obvious that Nick did not want to talk to her.

At noon on Friday, KC left her office and took her research with her. She was unable to concentrate at work, anyway. She stopped at her apartment and threw some clothes into a bag, grabbed her backpack, and headed to her parent's house a day early, planning to finish her research in the peace and quiet of her father's office. Besides, she desperately needed to get her mother's advice on dealing with Nick.

***

"I'm home!" KC called as she set her bags down in the entry. No answer. Taking a deep breath, KC expected to find the scent of fresh baked cookies or pie. Nothing. She dropped her bags in her old room and walked through the empty kitchen to the French doors that led out to the backyard. Sitting on the old bench, his legs stretched out comfortably and her favorite tea mug in his hand, Nick was in the middle of a conversation with her father.

"Dad?"

"Oh, hi there, Honey. I did not expect you until tomorrow."

"I see that." KC did not address Nick, because he seemed to be totally ignoring her and she refused to be the first one to speak. "Where is Mom?"

"Oh, she had a late lunch with her book club. A book signing or something. She should be home soon."

"Okay. I'll be in your office, working."

"Fine." With that quick dismissal, her father turned back to Nick as if she were not even there.

The door slammed loudly behind her as she went back into the house through the office door. No one seemed to notice.

He is my Dad. I can't believe Nick has hijacked him like this!

KC turned on the computer in the office and pulled out a new notebook and a pen from the center drawer of the desk. She deliberately turned off all thoughts of Nick, and focused on the information she was seeking. Finding birth records from Sacramento. Within minutes, she was totally engrossed in her research. There were several hospitals in the area, but the one closest to the address she had found for Caroline, which also had a brand new maternity ward back then, was Mercy General Hospital. Now for finding the record of births for that hospital for December 24, 1954. Hours had passed without finding what she was searching for, and KC finally decided to give up for the day. She turned off the computer, and closed the little notebook.

The house was quiet, except for the sounds of pots and pans being put to use in the kitchen.

Mom!

Rounding the corner, she met a very unexpected and surprising sight. Nick had his shirt sleeves rolled up to his elbows, and was wearing her mother's blue apron over his jeans. Spaghetti sauce was simmering on the stove, and freshly cooked pasta was draining in a colander in the sink.

"What have you done with my mother?"

"Oh, hello there. I was just about to come and get you. Wash up for dinner, it will be ready in just a minute."

It's worse than I thought—he is my mother!

She washed her hands in the guest bathroom and sat down at the kitchen table.

"What have you done with my parents?"

"Oh, your mom came home shortly after you went into your dad's office to work. She did not want to disturb you. She was dressed up so nicely for her book club event, that your dad decided to take her out to dinner and a movie. They said not to expect them until late."

Nick served the spaghetti with some rolls, poured iced tea into the tall glasses that he had set out, removed his apron, and sat down next to her as if it was the most natural thing in the world.

KC started to speak, when Nick reached out for her hand, bent his head, closed his eyes, and thanked God for the food.

"Nick, we have to talk."

"Eat first, talk later."

During the delicious dinner, the conversation revolved around the weather and basketball and all of the usual discussions found around a family dinner table. They might have been an old married couple. The thought made KC blush, and she covered her reaction by helping herself to another roll. Nick smiled and passed the butter.

As if they had done this for years, KC cleared the table while Nick put away the leftovers, and then they washed the dishes together, chatting amicably.

This is so weird! Why am I enjoying myself?

Taking the dish towel gently out of her hand, Nick hung it on the refrigerator handle and led KC into the living room, sitting next to her on the couch.

"Now we can talk."

"Nick, I . . ."

"Me first. I was wrong to get angry with you at lunch the other day without giving you an opportunity to explain. Your dad told me that you are the most ethical, upright person he knows, and that I should be ashamed of myself for doubting you."

"Really? My dad said that?"

"Yes he did."

"He was wrong."

"Excuse me?"

"I came this close to giving up my ethics to keep my job." She indicated a space of just an inch between her fingers.

"Mr. Knitzer threatened your job?"

"Well, not exactly my job. My column."

"You have worked hard to get to where you are, I can understand your fear of losing it all now."

"It doesn't matter. What kind of a person am I for even considering publishing the name of someone who has kept her secret for so many years? To sell newspapers. To look good to my boss. To write a story that would garner nationwide attention."

"A good person, KC. Someone who recognizes what is right and what is wrong, and chooses right."

KC started to say more, ready to confess that she still was not sure what she would do with this story, but Nick cut her off with a kiss. "You were saying?"

"I forget." KC leaned in for a kiss of her own, and all conversation ceased.

Nick stroked her cheek gently with his thumb, his head resting against hers and his arm reassuringly warm around her shoulders. "You know what I want, don't you?"

"Oh yes!"

KC smiled and stood up, pulling Nick up with her. She led him silently away from the living room, and into the kitchen.

"Ice cream?"

"Ice cream."

Her parents found them there a little while later, indulging in a second bowl of ice cream and some chocolate chip cookies that they had found in the freezer.

TWENTY-EIGHT

Another Monday morning found KC awake early, still smiling from her wonderful weekend with Nick and her parents, and still wired from the unbelievable amount of sugar that she had consumed.

No more sugar. Not today. Maybe not ever!

Settling for a nice, hot cup of tea and a toasted, stale bagel, she sat at her computer and began anew her search for the birth announcements from Sacramento's Mercy General Hospital. Several hours went by as she followed link after link. No, not there, not that page either—yes! There they were, scanned in from some paper copies somewhere and uploaded onto an obscure website. The words were a little fuzzy, but readable.

Born December 24, 1954:

- Boy, 7 lb 13 oz 5:15 am
- Boy, 5 lb 15 oz 6:30 am
- Girl, 6 lb 3 oz 11:47 am
- Twin girls, 4 lb 8 oz 12:45 pm and 4 lb 12 oz 1:05 pm
- Boy, 8 lb 7 oz 2:35 pm
- Girl, 5 lb 10 oz 5:47 pm
- Girl, 6 lb, 17 oz 11:30 pm

There were three baby girls born on that date, not counting the twins. She made careful notes in her new notebook.

Now to find out what hospital Caroline might have gone to if she was staying with her aunt, as she mentioned in her diary.

Aunt Coral, for whom Caroline might have been loosely named, lived in Tucson. Further research showed that she had not moved there until the mid-1960s. So, where did she live in 1954 when Caroline was pregnant?

The ringing of the doorbell broke her train of thought. She went to the door impatiently and looked through the peephole. Nick stood smiling on the other side, holding a brown paper bag.

"Come in. What a nice surprise!"

"I just couldn't leave you to do all of this fun research on your own. Things are slow at work since the crews are now off for the winter season. I figured you could use some help, and some food."

"Not sugar?"

KC was sure that Nick looked a little green at just the mention of it. She peaked into the bag. "Cheese-steak sandwiches. Perfect!"

She placed the sandwiches on plates and filled two glasses with ice water.

"I was just looking for Aunt Coral. Tucson is out. She did not move there until a decade later."

"Coral, Coral. That name sounds familiar. Where are the copies of the old newspaper articles you got from the Sacramento Library?"

They poured over the papers for more than an hour, spreading them out over the small floor in her apartment.

"Got it!"

***

Coral Robbins, Aunt to Caroline and Dorothy Smith, has joined their household for the fall season, as Senator Smith travels to Europe to explore options to expand his business. Ms. Robbins, of Marysville, expects to be in Sacramento through the new year.

***

"Wow! What a memory you have there, Fireman! So, according to the maps on my tablet, Marysville is about an hour from Sacramento. It is a relatively small town, and a logical place to send Caroline and still be close to home. KC spent a few moments looking up Marysville hospitals on her tablet. So Caroline could have delivered her baby at Rideout Memorial Hospital, in Marysville. Or perhaps she just came back to Sacramento."

"Did you find out anything about births in Sacramento from Dec 24?"

"Yes, here is the list. Three girls might be a possible match."

Nick was silent as KC performed more of her Internet search magic, not wanting to interrupt her train of thought.

"It does not appear that Marysville had any maternity facilities back then. It is more likely that her aunt brought her back to Sacramento. Her daughter could be one of the three babies on the list."

"Now we have to find aunt number two, from right here in Portland, Oregon. What do you have so far, KC?"

"I was able to get a name from her mother's family tree, Marie Redmond. Unfortunately, that is her maiden name. I have no idea if she was married."

"Okay, you search for marriage licenses and I'll go back through the copies of the newspapers again."

They each worked in companionable silence, with the rustling of the pages from the newspapers and the clicking of the keyboard the only sound, except for an occasional backfire from the garage next to the apartment.

"Lean back." Nick stood behind KC and rubbed her shoulders. "How about a short break and a little fresh air?"

The rain had let up, and the sun was peeking out from around the clouds, casting a golden glow as they made their way down the street to the little park on the corner. The wet swings and slides sat empty in the late afternoon. An old man with a little white furry dog, both wearing red tartan plaid coats, walked together on the soggy grass. KC and Nick strolled hand-in-hand past the dripping trees, and along the empty baseball field. At the corner food truck, they purchased two burritos and made their way around the block and back to the apartment.

"Hmm, that was nice. I'll make us some hot tea to go with our gourmet dinner. My hands are cold."

"Hey, don't complain. I have it on good authority that these are the best burritos in town."

"You won't find me arguing with a burrito expert!"

When the giant burritos were finished, they took their tea back into the living room and sat on the couch with KC's tablet on her lap where they could both see the results as she continued her search.

About an hour later, KC sighed and closed the tablet. "I'm starting to go cross-eyed looking at this screen. I think I am going to have to put the rest of the research off until tomorrow."

"That works for me. What time do you want me here?"

"I thought you had to work."

"I took the rest of the week off. When do you want me to come?"

"I have to get my column finished first. Eleven okay?"

KC stood and pulled Nick up with her. She couldn't resist a little kiss, followed by a slightly bigger kiss, which led to a whopper of a kiss.

"I'm going. Now. Well, maybe just one more."

KC ducked out of Nick's grasp, laughing, and opened the front door. "Goodnight."

Nick leaned down and snuck in one more peck on the cheek, then went down the stairs.

***

On the Lookout with KC Adams

October 4

Our time together exploring the fire lookouts is over. You have been with me from my adventures on the mountain, through the fire, and as we explored the interesting lives of those who watch over our land and protect us every summer.

Before we leave the lookouts, I would like to take you back to Iliana and my run-in with the bat. We will bypass the actual frenzied battle with the winged creature, and review what happened next.

"The board beneath my feet broke, sending me down onto the bed with one leg through to the floor at the bottom, and then the bat flew nonchalantly out of the door.

"I extricated myself from the bed and quickly closed all of the windows and the doors in case he changed his mind. I then pulled back my sleeping bag and the thin mattress and surveyed the damage. The main piece of lumber that held up the frame was still attached to the wall. Most of the lattice of wooden cross bars were still solid. But one section of wood had been purposely cut and then just set back in place. I had not broken the bed at all, just displaced this one section.

"As I tried to put everything back into place, I noticed something red in the opening under the bed. Laying in an uncomfortable and unnatural position, I managed to reach my arm down through the hole and pulled out an old book. Faded, and layered with years of dust, I had discovered what appears to be a very old diary. Could it be the journal of a lookout from generations ago?"

Today I share with you the beginning of a mystery. This old, red, diary was indeed from a past fire watcher. The woman who wrote it opened up her heart on the pages of that little book, and my own heart felt the pain of her losses and the joy of her accomplishments. There were no names and no dates.

Each week, you and I will explore some pages from the diary and solve the mysteries it contains together.

Until next week,

KC Adams

***

The knock on the door came just as KC pushed the send button on the newspaper website. She unplugged her tablet and tucked it in her backpack, then grabbed her coat and her umbrella and opened the door.

"Are we going somewhere?"

"Yes. The library."

"Another library?"

"Don't whine. I'll drive. I found out that they have the records we are looking for just a few miles away. The Internet has not been our friend here. It's time to do it the old-fashioned way."

"Hold on, Aunt Marie, we're coming!"

KC punched Nick in the arm as she walked past. He grinned and followed her down the steps.

The Multnomah County Central Library was a massive, old, brick building. It had huge arched doorways and windows, and an impressive amount of well-maintained greenery surrounded the building.

KC and Nick made their way to a long table, where KC unpacked her tablet and notebook, draped her jacket across the back of a chair, and headed for the reference counter. The man behind the counter looked so much like the person who had helped them in the Sacramento library, that KC did a double-take.

"Do you see that guy?" Nick whispered loudly in her ear.

"Hush."

The microfiche of the old newspapers and county records and the reader were in a back corner, so KC and Nick moved their things from the long table to a smaller one in the back.

Nick sat quietly, reading some historical records from Portland, while KC focused on her old newspaper search.

"Look at this," she whispered.

"No one can hear us clearly back here."

"Marriage licenses from the early 1950s. Marie Redmond and Clive Keys, married October 21, 1952."

"Cool! I'll get online on your tablet and see if anything pops up for Clive Keys or Marie Keys."

"Okay." They worked in companionable silence for a while.

"Hey!"

"What?"

"Look under obituaries from June 1953. It looks like Clive was killed in Korea."

KC pulled some microfiche cards from the files and after some searching, she called out. "You were right!"

"Hush! We are in a library."

"Oh, no one can hear us back here. It seems that they met while Clive was on leave from the Army, and he went back to Korea, only to be killed just a month before the war ended."

"Poor Aunt Marie."

"Yeah, well, it looks like she never remarried or had children. I found a newspaper article that mentions her accepting an award for her late husband in July of 1954. So we know she was still here. Caroline could have come to Portland while she was pregnant."

"Can you access hospital birth records here?"

"I'm on it!"

"Excuse me, could you two please keep your voices down?" The woman who spoke in an exaggerated whisper was wearing a brown pantsuit that matched her brown glasses and her short, mouse-brown hair, along with an official library name badge.

KC apologized and got back to her search silently. Nick buried his face in a book and tried not to laugh out loud. The librarian, mollified, went back to her desk.

"Let's go. I found the birth information from several hospitals in the area. Multnomah County Hospital, and Doctor's Hospital each had one baby girl born on Dec 24, 1954."

"Good work. Can we eat lunch now?"

KC laughed. "I love you!"

It just slipped out, but once said, could not be taken back again. She looked up to see if Nick had even heard her.

He was standing right in front of her. He gently took her face in his hands, and looked directly into her eyes.

"I love you too."

Then he kissed her. Right there in the library.

TWENTY-NINE

It is strange how three tiny words can change things. Love itself can cause a heart to flutter, a stomach to tighten, a sigh to escape. But love declared? That takes it away from an internal knowing to something you can shout to the world.

KC and Nick found their entire relationship changed the moment the words were uttered. The nightly phone calls resumed, and they spent every possible moment together. She did not second-guess his feelings, and he did not feel the need to tread lightly.

"How was work today?"

"Ugh! Boring paperwork, as usual this time of year. Tomorrow I am going out with a field crew to cut some trees off of a trail."

"Did they come down in that big rainstorm?"

"Yeah, it happens every year. How is your next column coming?"

"I have been so busy on the Internet trying to find out information about the babies, that I haven't even started it. Maybe tomorrow."

"I love you."

"I love you too."

***

On the Lookout with KC Adams

October 11

Today we begin to unravel the mystery of the red diary together. Are you ready?

As with any mystery, the best place to start is at the beginning. We first need to determine if the writer was a woman or a man. The beautiful handwriting and poetic nature of the writing seems to indicate that it was a woman.

"As I sit in my new home on top of the world, with the clouds and the birds as my neighbors, and the flowers and

trees as my décor, may the words come easily, and may my heart and soul be calmed by the writing of them."

As you will see as we delve deeper into the pages of the diary, the writer was indeed a woman.

Next, we should establish when the diary was written. Not a single date was included in the little book. I asked each person that I interviewed for my columns on Iliana lookouts if they had ever seen the diary before. No one had.

I know that some of you are thinking of forensics, perhaps determining the age of the paper or the ink. Unlike a television show, the clues do not come quite that easily in real life. The determining factor in this case was actually the impeccable memory of a couple whom you may remember were fire watchers in the 1950s — the Johnsons. They shared with me that the bed where I found the diary was built in 1953. And so we know that this must have been written after that. They also recalled a young woman who had been the lookout for the one summer that they had taken off during the decade that they had occupied that position. The year? 1955.

The mystery begins to be revealed. The book was written by a young woman in 1955.

Her words tell the story of a woman who came to Iliana to grieve the loss of her true love in an accident, and the loss of her child, surrendered for adoption. Read some excerpts from the diary below:

"My heart is still heavy with sadness, but the good rest and this quiet, meditative place will heal the wounds with time.

"I was thinking of my love again today, and remembering his red hair and crooked smile and sweet nature.

"I held her for just a moment, but I loved her."

Do you feel her pain? Next week I will share more from the diary of this young woman, and we will continue to unravel a mystery that has been hidden for many years.

Until next week,

KC Adams

***

On Sunday, KC went to church with Nick for the first time. His church, housed in an old-fashioned, little country building, packed a modern, energetic, spiritual punch. The music was loud and enthusiastic, the people friendly and warm, the message to-the-point and heart-felt. It was not at all what KC expected. The church in her hometown still boasted a pipe organ, and old hymns were sung with quiet reverence. The church that she had been attending in the city was somewhere between the two. Yet the message at all three churches was the same. In fact, the Bible verse from Nick's church was identical to the one read in her church the previous week. *Romans 10:9 That if thou shalt confess with thy mouth the Lord Jesus, and shalt believe in thine heart that God hath raised him from the dead, thou shalt be saved.*

So simple, KC thought. Why had she struggled with her faith for so long? After Derrick's death, she had turned her back on God. Yet, He had never let go of her. Did Caroline Smith's faith survive so many years in the cutthroat business world? How would she react to KC when she approached her about her child? Was all of this research for nothing?

It is if I don't find little Sara. Back to work!

KC decided to start with Portland. Since she lived there, it was practical, and a logical choice. If Senator Smith had been so careful to hide his daughter's pregnancy, it would seem reasonable to send her as far away as possible.

The names were easy to find from an online source that listed birth announcements from the newspapers from that date.

- Multnomah County Hospital, girl, 7 lb 6 oz, Dorinda, to Lucinda and Dorian Jones.
- Doctor's Hospital, girl, 6 lb 10 oz, Sophia, to Juanita and Carlos Vazquez.

The second listing seemed unlikely, since adoptions were usually kept within the same ethnicity back in the '50s. Prepared to make sure she covered every possibility, KC spent the next hour researching the Vazquez family. She found a wedding photo of Sophia from 1975. The beautiful woman with the crown of daisies around her dark hair was not the red-headed Sara of the diary. KC crossed her name off of the list in the little notebook.

Finding Dorinda seemed to be the biggest challenge. KC worked well into the night, searching out every Jones lead that she could find. The following evening, she was still hard at work, and no farther along in her research.

Nick called at the usual time, to find a frustrated KC.

"Did you stop to eat dinner?"

"I had some cold cereal a while back."

"I had a hot roast beef sandwich at the diner."

KC's stomach growled on cue. "Okay, I'll scramble a couple of eggs. That's the best I can manage right now."

"I get it. How is the research going? You said that you had a lead earlier, on a Dorinda Jones who taught at Multnomah High?"

"Yes, but I could not find anything else about her online."

"Why don't I take tomorrow off and we can check out the library."

"Do you think they will let us in?"

Nick laughed. "We will probably need to wear a disguise."

The next morning Nick picked KC up right on time, and they headed to the library. They were waiting on the steps when the doors were opened by the stern-faced woman who had quieted them on their previous visit. As they passed through the entry on their way to the reference area, they did not see the little smile that appeared on the face of the woman in brown. Or notice the red rose tucked into the lapel of her jacket. Could love be contagious?

A careful search of the bookshelves dedicated to the high school, led to the old yearbooks. Nick started with 1970, and KC began with 1990.

"Got it!" they called almost in unison.

"Quiet!"

"I found her photo from 1977." KC's voice was a contrite whisper.

"And I found her photo from 1990."

They compared the photographs. Dorinda Jones was a young, fresh-out-of-school English teacher in 1977. She had red hair and a cute freckled face. In 1990, her photo pictured a slightly more mature woman, and one of the group pictures clearly showed a wedding ring.

"Perhaps she kept her maiden name since she was already an established teacher. Whatever the reason, it has made it easier for us."

"Can I help you find something?" A gray-haired man with round wire-rimmed glasses came down the aisle where the yearbooks were located.

"I'm sorry, were we being too loud?"

"Oh, not at all. I don't work here anyway. I am just here doing some research on Multnomah High history for an article I am writing."

"So, are you familiar with the teachers from the high school?"

"Oh yes. I was the math teacher there for many years. Dan Brought here."

They shook hands and KC continued.

"Well you may be able to help us, then. We are looking for information on Dorinda Jones."

"Why don't you just ask her yourself?"

"Excuse me?"

"She is retiring this year, and they are holding a party for her at the school cafeteria this Friday evening at six."

"Would it be okay if we just showed up?"

"Sure, the party is open to the public. She taught so many students over the years, I suspect the place will be packed."

"Thank you so much Mr. Brought. You have no idea how helpful you have been!"

***

Friday evening could not have come soon enough for KC.

Tonight, I may meet Caroline's daughter!

KC changed clothes three times before settling on a blue flowered shirt, a denim skirt, and some navy flats. Nick was five minutes late and she was too nervous to care.

They arrived at the high school promptly at six, thanks to less traffic then they had expected. The parking lot was jammed, and Nick finally found a spot clear in the back corner.

"Thank goodness I wore flats or this walk would have killed me."

"Good plan. I expected to see those new red high heels that you bought the other day."

"Yeah, well, I thought about it. But Caroline was so petite, I expect Dorinda will be as well. I do not want to be looking down on her when I tell her about her birth mother."

"Hey, you are getting way ahead of yourself on this, KC. We don't even know if she is Caroline's daughter, or even if she was adopted at this point."

KC sighed. "You are right, as usual. I hate that, by the way."

"The fact that I am always right?"

"You are not *always* right. Just most of the time." The last part was a mere whisper.

"I did not hear that. Could you repeat it?"

"Look, Nick, we're here."

KC entered the large cafeteria to find a huge crowd of people. The noise of so many people talking at once hurt her ears, and she pictured this place at lunchtime every day, filled with a large group of boisterous teenagers. Nick reached for her arm and pointed toward the front of the room.

Dorinda Jones was the center of attention, sitting on a large chair that had been decorated to look like a throne, surrounded by generations of students and their children, wishing her well on her retirement. It took a little maneuvering for KC to get to a location where she could get a good look at her. The freckles had faded with the years, but Dorinda's red hair was unmistakable, despite the gray that was streaked throughout.

"They have ice cream." Nick spoke into her ear.

She smiled up at him. "Okay, let's go get some ice cream. We're going to have to wait until this crowd thins out before we can talk to her anyway."

"What?" The noise had increased to a din.

"Yes. Ice cream!"

It was nearing eight before enough people had left to enable KC and Nick to even get close to the new retiree.

"You two are not my students."

"Uh, no, we are not."

"I never forget a face."

"My name is . . ." KC was cut off by a small group of people who came to say goodbye before leaving.

THE STORY OF THE YEAR

"Hang out for a while." Dorinda spoke to KC loudly in her authoritative voice, then turned with a smile to say goodbye to the noisy group.

A half-hour later, the majority of the people had left, and Dorinda motioned for KC and Nick to come over.

KC put out her hand and introduced herself. "I'm KC Adams..."

"I know who you are! You write that column about the lookouts for the newspaper."

"This is Nick Evans." Dorinda stood up and shook hands with Nick as she looked him right in the eyes.

Uh, oh. And I was worried about wearing heels.

KC looked up at Dorinda, who stood nearly as tall as Nick. Caroline was described by the Johnsons and Kathryn's daughter, Beth, as being quite short. Perhaps not even five feet tall. And she also remembered the diary mentioning that Henry was not much taller. Her unwavering belief that this woman was Caroline's daughter began to falter just a little.

"I really enjoyed reading your column last Sunday. I love a good mystery."

"That's actually why I want to speak with you. Dorinda, is it possible that you were adopted?"

"Me? You think I am the baby from the diary?"

"You were born in Portland, Oregon, on Dec 24, 1954. The woman who wrote the diary had an aunt who lived in Portland, and she might have come here to deliver her child."

"Wouldn't that be fun? Unfortunately, there is no chance at all that I was adopted. Let me show you a photo I carry with me."

Dorinda sat back down and opened the large handbag that had been tucked under the chair. She rummaged around for a moment, and pulled out a photo wallet.

"This is my new grandson. Isn't he adorable?"

"Cute!"

"Let's see, here it is. This is a photograph of me when I was about twelve."

KC looked at a very young Dorinda, her freckles and braided red hair slightly faded on the old print.

"This is a photo of me with my sister and brothers taken the same year, standing next to our new station wagon."

Standing side-by-side were five tall, red-headed, freckled children, with Dorinda obviously being the oldest. They were unmistakably siblings. The same eyes, the same chins, the same long noses.

"Any doubts that we came from the same roots?"

"None." KC's sigh echoed in the nearly empty room.

"That's alright, Dear. You will find that baby and mother. I can't wait to read all about it in your column!"

"Thank you for your confidence. And congratulations on your retirement!"

The drive back home was quiet. Nick knew to let KC work things out quietly on her own, and he patiently gave her the space she needed. He pulled into the parking space in front of her apartment, and cleared his throat.

KC looked up and smiled, realizing that she was home.

"So, we are definitely getting somewhere by process of elimination. We now know that the baby was not born in Portland."

"Apparently not."

"Okay, then. Tomorrow I start on the list from Sacramento."

"No."

"No?"

"Tomorrow is Saturday, and we are both expected at your parent's house for a football marathon on TV in exchange for helping them rake leaves."

"We are? How is it that you talk more with my parents than I do?"

"I'm special. Your mom says so."

"You are special!" KC unbuckled her seatbelt and leaned over to give Nick a kiss. "I'll come by your place at eight and pick you up. I have some things I need to get from the attic while I am there, and they will fit better in the trunk of my car."

"What kind of things?"

"Oh, just some Christmas decorations and a few sweaters."

"Christmas! It's only the middle of October."

"I know, but it's never too early to start thinking about Christmas."

THIRTY

On the Lookout with KC Adams

October 18

Christmas. I know, it is still only the middle of October. But I want you all to think of Christmas this week, and what it means to you. Even if Christmas is not the holiday you celebrate, December is a time of year to get together with family and friends. It's a season of parties and dinners, of sending cards and making phone calls to those far away.

Is there someone special that you would love to be with this coming season? Perhaps a family member you have not seen in a long time?

I have a plan. As we unveiled part of the mystery of the diary last week, we found a young woman who had given up her baby for adoption. I believe that if we work together, we can find the identity of the mother and daughter and reunite them. In time for Christmas. Are you with me?

Now let's get to work in solving the rest of the mystery of the red diary. Here is an excerpt.

"Today I ventured down to the little spring, humming an old hymn as I went. Squirrels and birds chattered their own songs as I made my way down the path through the trees and brush. And there it was, standing just a few feet in front of the spring, big and intimidating and menacing. My heart pounded in my chest, but I did not back down. I am a purple dragon, after all. Who was this big, furry, creature to challenge me? I waved my arms and shouted 'This is my water! Go away!' The raccoon took off running and I have not seen him since."

Our mystery woman thinks she is a purple dragon? That has to be a clue. Help me out by writing to me on my social *media pages or sending me an email. We will solve this together.*

Until next week,

KC Adams

***

The hands of the clock were pointing straight up at midnight when KC sent off her column for the next week. This column was easy, since she had already solved that part of the mystery. When she began writing about finding the daughter, she just might need her readers help for real.

She set her alarm for 6:30 and climbed under the covers. Tomorrow was going to be a nice day with Nick and her family. She smiled briefly before gentle snoring took over.

***

Leaves flew everywhere when KC tackled Nick and sent him flying into the pile they had just so carefully created.

"No fair! You got me from behind."

KC smiled at him as he stood up with leaves clinging to his hair and his jacket. He looked irresistible. "All's fair in love and war."

"And this is?"

"Love. Definitely love."

Nick's kiss was tender and gentle, and KC felt herself grow warm despite the definite autumn chill in the air.

"Hey, you two. Break it up."

"Hello, Dad. Did you come to help?"

"No, I came to supervise, and it looks like you need supervision."

"Who, me?" KC was still flushed from Nick's kiss.

"I'll help you guys get the leaves into the plastic bags before they end up back out on the lawn. Mom says that the food will be done in twenty minutes. Just in time for the game."

Nick grabbed a huge armful of leaves and stuffed them into the bag. "Will work for food."

The meal was delicious, as usual, made more so by the family that shared it. They sat in the living room, watching the football game as they ate pulled pork sandwiches, baked beans, coleslaw, chips and homemade dill pickles. Dessert consisted of a giant platter of assorted cookies.

KC looked around the room as she munched on a pecan shortbread square, and remembered many such days, sitting in front of the TV with her folks, knowing how much she was loved. She glanced over at Nick, immersed in the game, and wondered what it must have been like for him growing up in those foster care homes. Had he ever known moments like this one? He seemed to fit in so easily with her family. She briefly thought of what it would be like to marry Nick and raise a family of their own.

Slow down, KC. Slow way down.

Nick looked over at her at that moment and she blushed. He did not seem to notice, thank goodness.

When the game was over, KC and Nick went into the kitchen to do the dishes while her parents relaxed in the living room, watching one of their favorite home improvement shows.

Nick handed her a large tray to dry. "That was fun."

"Yes, it was. I'm glad that you are here."

"I feel like a part of this family."

"You are."

There was a brief moment of quiet, and Nick's eyes began to tear up. He seemed a little uncomfortable at showing that much emotion.

"I think my dad likes you best!"

Nick laughed, and the moment passed.

When the last dish was dry, they sat at the kitchen table and Nick helped himself to another chocolate chip cookie.

"Really? Where do you put all of that?"

THE STORY OF THE YEAR

"Let's talk about the story. What's next?"

"Sacramento. There were three baby girls born on that date. One of them must be Caroline's daughter."

"I hope so. You are risking a lot by writing about the story now, before you have all of the puzzle pieces."

"Don't I know it! I have a lot of research to do, but I am determined to figure this out. I have so much work ahead of me, and deadlines to meet. I just have to keep plowing ahead."

Nick reached out for her hand. "Would you like to pray about it?"

Pray about it. KC realized that she had just been pushing her way through this process without even a thought about asking God for help.

"I'm afraid that I have a long way to go in my faith. Yes, let's pray."

"Lord, we know that this diary was found for a reason. We ask for Your guidance as we try to reunite this mother and daughter."

Nick squeezed KC's hand. "Better?"

"Better."

***

KC woke early on Wednesday morning, the work ahead of her foremost in her thoughts. She had spent the past few days searching on the Internet for information on the three girls who had been born in Sacramento on Dec 24, 1954. So far, she had come up empty. What few leads that she had come across, did not lead anywhere.

She was working from home these days, where she could spread out the many pages of information that she had accrued and not worry about someone else tripping over them. The print-outs from the newspapers that she had made from the Sacramento Library were fanned out along the floor. The information she had collected about Caroline was stacked on her coffee table, right next to the plate of crumbs from her breakfast and her empty tea mug. Next to her computer, still in the tray on her printer, was the most recent information that she had downloaded from the online resources she had found. The Christmas decorations retrieved from her parent's attic were still sitting in big boxes on her couch.

The doorbell rang.

Great!

"Nick! This is an unexpected visit."

"I can see that." Nick stepped through the door and into the chaos.

"Well, this is how I work. You should see what the inside of my head looks like."

"I'll pass." He gave her a quick kiss on the cheek. "Any luck?"

"Nope. And I have to turn in my next column today. I can manage this one, but I will need something more before the first column in November is due."

"Can you type and ride?"

"In a car?"

"Yes, in a car. I do not have my horse with me today."

"Where are we going?"

"Sacramento. How fast can you pack a bag?"

"Really?"

"Yes, really. You sounded so frustrated when we spoke earlier this morning. I say, let's go to the place where it all happened."

"Have I ever told you how amazing you are?"

The drive to Sacramento took just over nine hours, with only a few short stops for gas and some lunch on the go. KC jumped into writing her column as soon as they were underway, and had it completed long before they reached the Oregon/California border.

"Read it to me."

THE STORY OF THE YEAR

***

On the Lookout with KC Adams

October 25

I want to thank all of you who responded to the mystery of the purple dragon in last week's column. If you recall, that is what our young woman called herself on one of the pages of the diary.

I looked into all of your suggestions, from video games to Medieval England. The winner appears to be several of you who suggested the mascot from a school. A special thanks to John, who identified the purple dragon as the mascot from Sacramento High School.

Here is another clue from the diary that helped.

"I was walking through Capitol Park, enjoying the flowers and the different varieties of trees, when a young girl came flying past me on a bicycle where Thirteenth Street crosses the park."

My research shows that almost every state has a Capitol Park. Yet when I added the name of the street to the name of the park, my search engine pointed right to Sacramento, California.

As I write this column, I am headed to California's capitol city, hoping to uncover information on the identity of the young mother and daughter.

November is just around the corner, and Christmas is not far off. The air had a hint of frost in it this morning, and it reminds me that our quest to reunite these two women is fast approaching.

How can you help this week? If you have adopted a child, or have been adopted yourself, let me know how you feel about this mission. I value your input.

Until next week,

KC Adams

***

"That is really good, KC."

"Thank you. That's it as far as our current research goes. I can't reveal the name of the mother in the column, and so I need to focus on finding the daughter."

"We'll find her. Together."

"Yes we will. Together."

They headed up into the mountains of southern Oregon, the freeway winding up and around, green, tree-lined slopes giving way to green, grass-filled valleys, only to reveal yet another rocky mountain around the next corner.

They stopped in Yreka for a quick lunch, where KC connected her tablet to the restaurant's Wi-Fi and sent in her column. They filled the tank with gas and headed south again. An early snow had fallen on the tops of the highest mountains. When Mt. Shasta came into view, the site took KC's breath away. This was way better than flying in so many ways. Nick was singing along with the tune on the radio, and even though he got most of the words completely wrong, KC had to smile at his enthusiasm. She felt warm and happy and loved.

"Wake up, sleepy. We're just a few miles away from Sacramento."

"Really?" KC stretched and rubbed her eyes. "I'm so sorry! I was not very good company."

"That's okay. I love to drive, and you needed to catch up on some sleep."

"Yes, I did."

"Well, now that you are up, can you check the driving directions and get the exit number?"

They settled into their hotel rooms, and met downstairs at the coffee shop for dinner.

"I can't believe that you are using your valuable time off to come all this way with me. Don't you have any vacations planned where you can better use your time?"

"I do have a big fishing trip with some buddies in the spring. But I have a lot of leave hours to use before the end of the year. Besides, any time I spend with you is like a vacation."

"Nice. Corny, but nice."

"I have something very important to ask you."

No! Now? Right here? In this coffee shop?

Nick grinned mischievously. "Could you please pass the salt?"

KC kicked him under the table.

***

It was a few minutes after noon when Nick interrupted KC as she sat at the microfiche reader in the library.

"Aren't you getting hungry?"

"Give me just ten more minutes."

Twenty minutes later KC packed up her tablet and tucked it into her backpack. Nick grabbed their jackets from the back of the chairs and they headed down the block to the nearest restaurant.

"Wouldn't you rather have a burrito?"

"No, this Thai food looks great. I am a man who appreciates many different cultures."

"Have you tried Thai iced tea before?"

"Yes. It's good, but very sweet."

"Like me?"

"Just like you."

The enticing scents filled the restaurant, and it was not long before their table was covered with plates of rice and vegetables, and spicy meat dishes. They settled for hot green tea, and enjoyed the feast quietly.

Nick looked down at his watch for the third time as KC lingered over her last cup of tea.

"Are we late for an appointment somewhere?"

"Not quite, but we do need to get moving."

"Where are we going?"

"I read today's local newspaper while you were researching the past, and there is a tea at a nearby garden in about a half-hour. I thought you might want to go."

"Do I look like a woman who needs more tea?"

"No, but you look like a woman who might want to hear Carol Smith speak to a group of business women at 3:00 today."

"Really?"

"Yes. Are you ready to go?"

"You just try and keep up!" KC grabbed her backpack and jacket and made her way out to the sidewalk. "Uh, which way are we going?"

"Right."

"Right!"

The charming little garden turned out to be a beautiful and charming good-sized maze, and Nick and KC found a few chairs in the back row just in front of a grouping of yellow and pink mums. They took their seats as quietly as possible, while a tall brunette was already in the process of introducing the guest speaker.

"And so with no further comments needed on my part, I give you Carol Smith."

The woman came to the podium and adjusted the microphone down to her level amid the scattered applause. She did not look like a woman in her 80s. She was dressed impeccably in a gray, tweed jacket and slacks, and an ice-blue silk blouse with a soft collar that framed her face. Her blonde hair was cut in a modern bob, and the small, gold, dangles at her ears matched the necklace that peeked out from behind the collar.

THE STORY OF THE YEAR

KC looked past the expensive clothing and jewelry and into Caroline's green eyes. From the back row she could see no emotion behind them, and although her voice was strong and her message professional, Caroline's words came across as practiced and somewhat cold. The moment she was done speaking, she turned and left the podium and was escorted out. So much for having an opportunity to speak to her.

"Well, Nick, what did you think?"

"She looks younger than I expected. But I sensed not one bit of emotion. You?"

"Yeah, I had the same impression. What happens when we contact her with information about her daughter? Will she even care?"

"We will never know if we don't find the daughter first."

"Right. Are you ready to head back to the library?"

THIRTY-ONE

The alarm went off annoyingly at seven, and KC hit the off button much harder than necessary to silence it. She and Nick had arrived back in the Portland area late the night before, and she was supposed to meet Mr. Knitzer at the office later that morning. She did not like being summoned to a meeting with an impersonal text, but he was the boss, after all. She really should have checked her email earlier. She might have been better prepared for the appointment. Or maybe not.

Dressed in a meeting-ready outfit, her backpack, still full of the research she had printed out in Sacramento, over her shoulder, KC grabbed an umbrella and headed out to the office. It was remarkable to think that she had been sitting in a sunny garden listening to Caroline Smith the previous afternoon, and now walking in the chilly rain in Portland less than twenty-four hours later.

Mug of tea in hand, KC wiped the crumbs off of her mouth from the donut she had snatched from the breakroom, and waited for the elevator to stop at the top floor.

"Come in, KC. Come in. Have a seat."

Mr. Knitzer did not get up, but just motioned her to a chair and turned his attention back to his computer screen.

KC waited quietly. Not patiently, but quietly.

"Take a look at this."

Mr. Knitzer turned his computer monitor toward her, and KC leaned forward and looked at an incredible number of social media messages sent to her newspaper account.

"All of these are responding to my question about reuniting the mother and daughter?"

"Yes, and this is just one site. How long has it been since you checked your email?"

"Just briefly a few days ago. I have been busy researching this story."

"Yes, yes, I understand. This story has garnered more interest than anything that you have written before. I am impressed. Yes, impressed. Can you imagine how many readers we will gain when you release the name of the mother?"

"About that . . ."

***

KC checked her voicemail again, but Nick had not replied to her message. No text, nothing. She sighed loudly and began to pace the floor in her living room, an activity made nearly impossible as she zig-zagged through the small space, trying not to step on the pages of research still spread out on the floor.

KC, don't be so stupid. He'll call when he can. Clean up this room, for goodness sake!

The tiny, two-drawer file cabinet under her desk was quickly filled with organized file folders of the newspaper printouts and the printed copies of the information that she had found on the web. She unloaded her backpack and organized the papers she had brought back with her from her most recent trip to the Sacramento library into neat piles on the coffee table. Once the floor and her desk was cleaned off completely, she opened the boxes of Christmas decorations that she had brought back from her parent's attic.

Humming 'I Need a Little Christmas' from the musical *Auntie Mame*, KC put the colorful garland that had once decorated the doorway in her childhood bedroom over the tiny mantel. She set a shiny red bowl of fake holly in the middle of her dining room table and adjusted the leaves. Placing a fat Santa on one side of her bookshelf, she pushed him up straight, only to have him lean sideways once again as soon as she let go. She finally gave up and left him leaning drunkenly against her copy of *A Christmas Carol*, which seemed appropriate enough. The snowmen salt and pepper shakers that had belonged to her grandmother were given a place of honor on her kitchen counter. The rest of the decorations were placed back in the boxes, and tucked in among the boots on the floor of her little coat closet.

Sitting down on the couch to survey the results, KC jumped a little when her phone rang.

"Nick! I have been waiting for your call."

"Sorry, Honey, I forgot to charge my battery and my phone was dead. I just plugged in at home and saw your messages. All of them. Is everything okay? Are you okay?"

"Yes, I'm fine. I just really need to talk to you."

"Do you want me to come over?"

"No, you have done enough driving for a while. Do you want to meet at that nice restaurant near your house?"

"Sure. How soon can you be here?"

"I'm in my car now, heading your way. Gotta go. I'll meet you in about thirty-five minutes."

Nick was already waiting, and he gave KC a much-needed hug and an impressive kiss. The restaurant was not too crowded, which was surprising. It was usually packed at the dinner hour. KC glanced at her watch to see it was just a little after five. They sat at a table in the back at Nick's request, and ordered the fish special and iced tea, anxious for the waitress to finish her job and leave them alone to talk.

"Tell me about the meeting with Mr. Knitzer. I assume that is what your messages were about?"

"Yeah, that's it exactly." Her expression was serious, without the hint of a smile.

"Talk to me, KC."

"He loves the columns that I have been writing. He showed me a boatload of responses from the readers on my question on adoptees contacting the birth parents and vice versa."

"Well, that's good. Right?"

"Yes and no. Of course, it is good to get the readers involved. And it appears we are gaining a large following, which sells papers."

"So the problem is . . . ?"

"Mr. Knitzer wants me to reveal the name of the mother."

"Oh."

"It's my fault for proclaiming loudly in that last meeting with him that this was a very high-profile woman. My conscience told me not to say it, but I blurted it out anyway."

"That's in the past. What did you tell him today?"

The waitress approached them with their salads, and they thanked her politely and waited for her to leave before resuming their conversation.

"I'm sorry to be so cautious, I'm just a little wary of saying something that could be overheard in public after that slew of photographs of us that appeared on social media without our knowledge or consent."

"I understand, KC. I did look so much better in those photos than you."

That little quip earned him her first smile of the evening.

"I told Mr. Knitzer that I was not going to compromise this woman's privacy to sell newspapers. He told me that we were in the business of selling newspapers."

"Hmm. He's right there. What did you say to that?"

"I remembered something that you said, and reminded him that we are not a tabloid, but a newspaper that 'cares about people'. That phrase is in our mission statement, but I never expected to use it to argue with my boss."

"Good job! Did he agree?"

"Tentatively. He said that if I could write about the reunion of the mother and daughter in a way that satisfied the readers, he would leave it at that. The thing is, if I don't find the daughter, or even if I do and Caroline refuses to meet her, I can't write the column I have promised my readers and my boss. I have really put myself and the newspaper in a bind if this story falls flat. My only option might be to reveal Caroline's identity."

"I thought we agreed that was not the right thing to do."

"I know, but I may not have a choice."

"You always have a choice, KC. What did your editor say next?"

"He asked if I had found the daughter yet, and I had to admit that I had not."

"Not yet."

"Yes, not yet."

"Was he satisfied with that?"

"I have until the Sunday before Christmas."

"Christmas is a long way out."

"It's closer than you think."

"Well, let's eat our dinner and get back to work then."

"You are amazing."

"I know."

***

The screen on her computer was becoming blurry as KC struggled to stay awake and finish reading the responses and comments from her readers. She had filled an entire notebook with those comments she thought might assist her in finding Caroline's daughter. She was in total awe of the help her readers had provided. A few of the people who had been adopted said that their adoptive parents *were* their real parents, and they had no desire to meet the woman who had given birth to them. A few birth parents were adamant that they wanted nothing to do with the unwanted child, and resented the fact that their privacy might be compromised. She took the time to respond to each of these, reassuring them that was not the case. Most of the responses were positive.

"I was adopted back in the 1960s when adoptions were still kept a secret. Now I am married and have adopted four children of my own. These were open adoptions, and the children have all had contact with their birth mothers over the years. There is room in their hearts for both of us."

"I have been looking for my birth mother for many years. I am sad that she apparently does not want to find me as well."

"My brother and I were reunited after twenty years of being raised in different families. Here is the website where anyone can put their information if they want to be found. I hope that this helps you find the writer of the red diary and her daughter."

That last message was one of several that included links to websites created to facilitate the process. KC was excited to look into them, but tonight she was just too tired.

The next morning, she made a strong pot of coffee and began to delve into the adoption websites. Several hours later, she hit the jackpot.

"I was born on December 24, 1954, at Sacramento's Mercy General Hospital. I weighed 6 lb 3 oz and was born at 11:47 a.m. I am looking for my birth parents and any possible siblings. Contact Jannice C. Randolf at . . ."

KC double-checked her notes from the Sacramento information. Yes! The time and weight matched the first girl listed perfectly. KC quickly responded to the email link provided, and then did a search for the name Jannice C. Randolf.

Oh, she's an author! Cool.

A list of published books popped up in her search engine, and KC clicked on the link that said 'new release'. The face of a beautiful woman graced the cover of the book entitled "Growing up Black in the Sixties". This woman, unfortunately, was not Caroline's daughter.

Just then, KC's laptop dinged the sound of a new email. She checked it right away.

"Thank you so much for responding to the adoption website message, but I have already been in contact with my birth father and a sister. I will take that message off as quickly as I can to avoid any further confusion. Good luck with your search. Jannice."

Despite the number of hours spent searching, the remainder of the day and a good portion of the following day led to no further clues, though the number of people looking for each other offered KC some hope.

Nick arrived with dinner-in-a-bag at six that evening, and they looked at the rest of the sites together. Some were obvious scams asking for money, but many were there to help. Most of the dates that people listed were much later than 1954.

"Do you want the last cookie?"

"No, help yourself."

"All of that information we found on our last trip to Sacramento gave you nothing?"

"Nothing. It may help us later, but not right now."

Nick crunched away on the cookie, his brow knit in earnest thought as they pondered the options. "Why don't you ask your readers for help?"

"They have helped."

"No, I mean, give them the actual date of birth, and ask them to help you find the daughter."

"That is an excellent idea! You are a genius, Nick Evans."

"I know."

"I can keep the data about the baby's weight and time of birth for the last two girls on the list to myself to weed out the wrong information."

"Good thought. You're pretty smart yourself, KC Adams. By the way, are you ever planning to tell me what the 'C' stands for?"

"Nope. Never. I'm excited to write my next column asking for the reader's help. I'll get right on it."

Nick stood up and closed the top of KC's laptop. "You'll get right on it tomorrow. Your boyfriend needs some attention now."

"Are you my boyfriend?"

Her question was met with a big kiss that left no doubt.

THE STORY OF THE YEAR

***

On the Lookout with KC Adams

November 1

The mystery of the red notebook is being revealed to us one clue at a time. Together, we have discovered that it was written in 1955, by a young woman from Sacramento. We found out that her true love died, and she gave up her baby girl for adoption.

I asked you last week if you had been adopted, or had given up a child for adoption, what you thought of the plan to reunite the mother and daughter in time for Christmas. Your response was overwhelmingly positive, and I am still going through your messages, reading each and every one carefully.

Today I reveal another clue that has brought us a very important piece of information.

Here is an excerpt from the diary:

"The sadness is not gone. It never will be. My baby is six months old today!"

The previous day she wrote:

"A family with eight children had managed to set their little tent on fire along with the brush and trees around it."

Research into the newspaper records from the summer of 1955 yielded this piece of an article:

"June 23, 1955. A family from nearby Jenson Creek was camping in the Huckleberry Campground when a candle accidentally set fire to their tent. None of the eight children were injured, and the fire was spotted from the Iliana Lookout Tower and reported quickly. The local fire crew responded immediately, and the Tent Fire was contained at just under ten acres."

Do you know what this means?

Now we have a birthdate to go with our location! Another clue to our mystery. The writer's baby was born on December 24, 1954, in Sacramento, California.

This week I am going to ask for help yet again from all of you, my loyal readers. I spent a good part of the past week doing intense research, now that I know the date, and have not been able to find anything. I am not giving up, but I am just one woman. But together, we are a force to be reckoned with.

Will you help me?

Until next week,

KC Adams

THIRTY-TWO

"Good grief! Look at this."

Nick leaned over toward KC as they sat side-by-side on the couch. She pointed to one of the messages she was reading on her tablet.

"I think I am the mother you are seeking. I gave up a baby for adoption in June of 1964. I don't remember if it was a boy or a girl. I was living in San Francisco at the time, and . . ."

"How many pages of explanation does this woman give?"

"Oh, there are about five pages or so. That's why she sent this in an email. Social media has limits on space."

"Any luck on that side of things?"

"Not really. It actually gets worse. Look at this message."

"I am the daughter you are seeking. Does this woman have a lot of money?"

"So, nothing helpful?"

"Not a single thing. I have been reading these responses all week long, and I have jotted down only about a half-dozen comments that had any substance. None of them panned out. Big zero, zip, nothing."

Nick put his arm around KC and kissed her on the cheek.

"Maybe my idea was not so genius after all?"

"No, I still think it is a good idea. I just have to wade through all the crazies first."

"What did you do about your column this week?"

"Oh, I wrote about finding the mother—without giving any names, of course. I am doing my best to do what I feel is right. I put in a few quotes from the diary. Would you like to read it?"

"Of course."

***

THE STORY OF THE YEAR

On the Lookout with KC Adams

November 8

A big thank you to all of you who took the time to write to me this week. I am still searching for the daughter who was born on December 24, 1954, and given up for adoption by a loving mother.

If you have any pertinent information that you think will help, please send me a message. I read each and every one.

The mystery of the diary took a turn for the better this week. Let's look at some things that could help determine the identity of the young mother.

Her summer spent at Iliana was a time of grieving and healing:

"Up on this mountain there are no distractions to keep my mind from focusing on the events of the past year."

She was a woman who was deeply in love:

"His memory will live on in my heart forever."

"Our love was not something to be ashamed of."

She loved her baby daughter with all of her heart:

"I crossed my arms over my empty body and remembered the child I carried there. I am alone."

"I held her for just a moment, but I loved her."

"She is better off with a real family. But I will never be the same again."

The sad, young mother left some clues in the pages of the old, red diary. Together we found out that she came from Sacramento, and that she was a lookout in 1955. I found out through searching the old records, that she used an assumed name when she applied to be a lookout, a fact that she confirmed in the diary. Although she never told us her real name, she mentioned the name of a friend. I found the daughter of that friend, and through her additional information, I was led to even more clues.

Now, I have something very important to tell you. I know the identity of the writer of the diary!

No, I am not going to divulge her name to you now. This secret was so important to her, that she did everything in her power to keep it private. I cannot, in good conscience, reveal what she so clearly wanted to remain hidden. I will tell you that she is a healthy and active woman in her 80s. I have not contacted her, and will not do so until I have the second piece of the mystery, the identity of the daughter.

The time is growing close to find the woman who was given up for adoption, and to reunite her with her mother in time for Christmas.

Are you still with me? Keep those helpful messages coming.

Until next week,

KC Adams

***

"What did you mean when you said *I'm not going to divulge her name to you now*? I thought you were going to keep Caroline's secret?"

"I'm just keeping my options open."

"Well, it's a great column."

"You think so?"

"I know so."

"Thank you."

"How about putting this away for today and going out for ice cream?"

"How is it that you don't weigh 800 pounds?"

"It's all muscle."

THE STORY OF THE YEAR

The cool, fall evening had just a hint of rain in the air as KC and Nick made their way along the sidewalks to their favorite ice cream shop. The lights from the store windows they passed reflected in the wet cement, glittering like white diamonds as they walked.

"I love this time of year."

"Me too. They are putting out the Christmas stuff already."

"Speaking of Christmas—are you aware that you have Christmas decorations in your apartment before Thanksgiving?"

"Yeah, it's kind of my thing. You'll get used to it."

They sat on the little metal stools in the ice cream shop and savored their dessert, as the rain began to fall again outside. Despite her frustration with the dead-ends on her search for the daughter, KC realized that she had never been happier.

"I could sit here with you like this forever."

Oh no! Did I just say that out loud?

"If you did, you would be the one who weighed 800 pounds."

The walk back in the pouring rain became more of a soggy sprint, and they were both thoroughly soaked by the time they made it to her apartment. After a squishy hug and a water-logged kiss goodbye at her doorstep, Nick left her dripping on the little mat inside her door with a big smile on her face.

Hot bath, warm fleece pajamas, and bed.

KC did not turn her computer back on before she headed for that bath and bed, and thus did not see the new email that had come in while she was out with Nick.

***

The next morning, as she was about to put her tablet into the backpack again and head to the office, she decided to check her messages before leaving. Perhaps the rain would let up just a bit if she waited a few minutes longer.

"Dear Ms. Adams,

I have been out of the state, and have just now read your past columns on the diary that you found at the Iliana Lookout. I was born on December 24, 1954, in Sacramento. I have always known that I was adopted, but have never felt the need to contact my birth mother. However, with the passing of my parents in the past few years, it has crossed my mind. I may be the person you are looking for. I am only going to be in this area for a few days, but I would be happy to meet with you. Call me at your convenience at . . .

Doris Smith"

Now wouldn't that be funny, if her name is also Smith?

KC picked up the phone and dialed the number from the message immediately. Doris Smith answered on the third ring, and they made arrangements to meet at one of the better restaurants for lunch.

KC hurried back into her bedroom to change into a more appropriate outfit, and left a message for Nick on his cellphone. She gathered her backpack, her coat and her umbrella, and made her way to the office, humming the entire way.

The morning went slowly, as KC met briefly with Mr. Knitzer to give him an update on her progress, then waded through more emails and messages that were of no help to her search.

Maybe my search is over. I'm about to find out.

The restaurant was more glamorous than she had even envisioned, having read a raving review about it a few months earlier. KC quietly checked her wallet to make sure she had enough to pay for lunch in such a nice place. White linen tablecloths covered the tops of the iron tables, while richly padded chairs in slate gray matched the napkins which were folded like swans at each place. The hostess seated her at a small table, and KC fidgeted with the edge of the swan-shaped napkin and sipped ice water as she waited for Doris Smith to arrive. A tall, blonde woman entered and made eye contact with KC, then smiled regally and followed the hostess to the table. After the introductions and handshakes, Doris made herself comfortable, ordering white wine and relaxing into the comfortable chair.

"So tell me about this mysterious diary. You wrote that you found it under the bed?"

"Yes, and I nearly broke my leg in the process."

Doris smiled politely, but her expression seemed rather chilly. Where had KC seen that expression recently? Oh yes! At the garden, in Caroline Smith's cool green eyes. KC looked at Doris more intently, and noticed that her eyes were dark blue.

"Well, that sounds like quite an adventure. Shall we order?"

The menu had the prices in little, tiny print next to the selection, and KC had to tilt the page toward the light to read it. She recalled the amount in her wallet, and ordered the smallest salad listed. Doris ordered the salmon.

"You mentioned that you always knew that you were adopted. Did your parents ever tell you anything else?"

"No, we never really discussed it. It was not until after they passed away in the last few years that the thought of my birth mother even crossed my mind."

KC had just spent weeks reading messages from people who were adopted and had always wondered about their birth parents. None of them had indicated this amount of apathy. How strange.

"Can you tell me some more details about your birth?"

Just then their lunch arrived, and KC nibbled slowly on her tiny, though artistic, salad, while Doris ordered another glass of wine and enjoyed her salmon, risotto, and sautéed vegetables.

KC tried again. "Do you have a copy of your birth certificate?"

"Oh, yes, of course I do. I made a photo copy for you. You may take it with you."

"Thank you." KC glanced at the document quickly, then tucked the paper into her backpack.

"Well, I must go now. I have a hair appointment. You may reach me at the phone number you used earlier. I am only in town for a few days. I would like to get this matter settled before I have to leave."

"I will call you soon."

"Goodbye, and thank you for lunch."

With that, Doris Smith picked up her elegant handbag and jacket and glided out of the restaurant.

"Your check, miss."

KC looked down at the check and up at the expectant waiter. She reached into her wallet and pulled out the credit card that she reserved for emergencies.

***

"She stuck you for lunch?"

"It all happened so fast."

"Was the lunch her idea, or yours?"

"I think we just kind of agreed on it together."

"But she chose the restaurant."

"Yes she did."

Nick patted KC's arm and smiled at her. "Are you finished with dinner, or would you like the other half of my bread?"

"I was famished! That salad wouldn't have kept a bunny alive!"

"Ice cream?"

"No, I'm good. Broke, but good."

"How much *was* that lunch?"

"Too much. Way too much."

"Come on, poor little reporter, I'll drive you home. I'd like a chance to look at that birth certificate."

Seated in her warm and well-lighted kitchen, KC kicked her shoes off under the table and pulled out the photocopy of the birth certificate from her backpack. It had the official seal, or so it seemed, since it was hard to tell with a black and white photocopy. The hospital logo was correct, according to what they found online. The date and time and baby's weight were just right. Girl, 6 lb, 17 oz 11:30 p.m.

Nick looked the paper over carefully, and broke into a grin. "Do you see anything wrong here?"

"Uh, no. It looks fine to me."

"Look at the weight."

"It's the same as the weight from the old newspaper announcement that I found on the Internet."

"KC—17 ounces? There are only 16 ounces in a pound."

"Oh, yes, of course you are right. Well, maybe the birth certificate is wrong and the newspaper got it off of the birth certificate."

"Or maybe our Doris Smith got it from the same website newspaper information that you got online, and made the birth certificate to match."

"You think she faked this? Why would she do that?"

"I don't know, but I trust you to find out. You're a good reporter. Is there anything else about her that seemed off?"

"She was kind of tall."

"Tall?"

"Tall and blonde."

"Oh, well that settles it. She is obviously a fake."

KC laughed for the first time since lunch. If Doris Smith was an imposter, she would find out.

***

The following morning, KC was up early and well into her research on the Internet when Nick called.

"I have a friend who is an ex-cop. Just retired a year ago. He does a little detective work on the side. I told him about this, and he has offered to help."

"That might be a really good idea. I have done some research into birth certificates from the old Mercy General Hospital, and the copy I have just looks off. Not quite lined up. I called the county clerk and asked if it was possible to have an incorrect weight number like that on an official document, and she said that it was highly unlikely."

"But nothing solid."

"No, but here is the strangest part. I looked up Doris Smith on all of the social media sites and she is not there. I even paid one of those sites to find someone's email address, and got nothing else. The email address that Doris used to contact me had just been created the previous day."

"You have a phone number to reach her?"

"Yes."

"Set up a morning meeting at ten at our favorite coffee place. They have a wall of big windows. Sit at one of the front tables and I'll have my friend outside."

"Ooh, this feels like a TV mystery movie. I can keep the conversation going while he checks her out."

"You just be careful, KC. This is not television. And we don't know why someone would go to such great lengths to perpetrate a hoax. Do you think she knows, somehow, about Caroline?"

"Maybe not Caroline, exactly. But perhaps she senses a payday coming. I will not let that happen."

***

The following morning at ten, KC waited at one of the front tables of the coffee shop, nursing a tall caramel macchiato, while she waited for Doris to show up. She could not see Nick or his friend from the large window, but she was confident that they were out there.

"I'm sorry that I'm late. I'm not used to this part of town. What do they offer here?"

"The menu is up front. I'll wait here while you get yourself something."

You are not going to pull that on me twice, lady!

Settled in at the front table, KC gave Doris back the copy of the birth certificate. She had made a copy for herself, of course.

"Thank you so much for providing that. The date, time, and weight all match a baby girl from the list I found in my research."

"Well, of course it does. When do you propose to orchestrate the reunion?"

"I'm still working on it."

"Well, as I told you, I am only in town for a few days. I can extend it for perhaps a week, but no longer."

"Yes, you told me. Doris, why haven't you asked anything about your mother?"

"My mother? Oh, my birth mother? I am still getting used to the idea. But I am excited at the prospect of meeting her, of course."

Smooth. Emotionless, but smooth.

"I have just a few more details to check, and then I will let you know."

"I am thrilled at the thought of finally meeting her," Doris said in a flat, cool, voice.

The bell on the front door of the coffee shop rang sharply, and KC glanced up to see a man walk in wearing a dark suit and a beige trench coat. Her mind went straight to one of the many TV movies she loved to watch, and she sat up straighter and kept a wary eye on him. He went to the front and ordered a coffee, then made his way straight to their table.

"Doris Smith?"

"Yes, I'm Doris Smith."

"Then you must be KC Adams." He reached out his hand, but KC ignored the gesture.

"And you are . . . ?"

"Ralph Smooker, of 'The Evening Gossip.' I assume you have seen the show?"

"I know what it is." KC avoided adding her definition—Tabloid TV.

"Doris and I spoke a few days ago, and she has promised us exclusive coverage of the reunion between the mother and daughter that you have been writing about in your newspaper column. You have an incredible amount of traction on social media. We are *very* interested in getting this story."

"I'm sure you are, but you *do* understand that I work for the paper? This is *my* story."

"Yes, of course it is. I am offering you the opportunity to advance your career, from a simple newspaper columnist, to a reporter on national television. I assure you that we can offer a much higher salary than you are currently getting. It would be financially profitable for you both to give us the opportunity to cover this touching reunion."

"Thank you for your offer, but . . ."

"Don't say no just yet! I am also authorized to offer you a nice bonus!"

"Not gonna happen."

Just as KC was thinking of a few additional words to add to her refusal, the front door opened again, and Nick came in with a stocky man with gray hair and a determined look in his dark eyes. They came straight to her table.

"Hello, Maggie."

Doris Smith squirmed in her seat, looking frantically for a way to leave. Her exit was blocked by the window on one side and the gray-haired man with his hand firmly on her shoulder on the other side.

"KC, meet Maggie Johansen, a con-artist and a very slippery felon. Sorry, Maggie, you should not have come back into this state."

A police car with flashing lights pulled up in front of the coffee shop, and two uniformed officers got out. Within just a few minutes,

Maggie Johansen, alias Doris Smith, was handcuffed and placed in the back seat of the cruiser.

Ralph Smooker just stood there looking puzzled, but quickly regained his composure. He reached into his coat pocket, produced a business card, and handed it to KC.

"We are still interested in covering your story, KC. The offer of a job still stands; you'd make an awesome TV reporter!"

THIRTY-THREE

"You aren't really considering the job offer from that sleaze-ball, are you?"

"I don't know; it would be a lot more money. I could change my lovely view of the auto shop for a view of some trees or the river."

Nick saw the look of teasing in her eyes, and his shoulders dropped down several inches as the tension left him.

KC poured more iced tea for each of them, and they both reached for the same piece of fried chicken, sparking a laugh and an impromptu kiss. The laughter was short-lived, as they began to discuss the options left to them to solve the rest of the mystery and find the adopted daughter.

"I did not like Doris—rather, Maggie, from the very first. But I have to admit, I was happy when I thought the searching was over."

"I know. So, the search continues. What leads do you have to work with?"

"None."

"None?"

"As in, not a single lead, clue, promising Internet link, nothing."

"Have you read all of your emails and social medial messages?"

"Not yet. There are still a bunch showing up, and I stopped looking until after I met with Doris Smith. Now I am behind."

"Well, let's work on those together after I finish the last wing."

"We can work on it together after *I* finish the last wing." KC grabbed the final piece of chicken from the plate and made a dramatic spectacle of eating it, licking her fingers at the end.

Settled down on the couch after lunch was over, with the tablet between them, KC and Nick spent the afternoon reading everything sent by the readers. There were a few new website addresses, and Nick jotted them down in the notebook. Only one email showed promise, but the weight and time were wrong, and further research showed that the woman had been born in a different city in California.

KC stretched, and closed her tablet. "I'll check out those websites tomorrow. Today, I need to concentrate on finishing my column."

"What are you going to write about?"

"Oh, I'll stall for another week. I will write about the experience with Doris, for sure. The following week I have a Thanksgiving column to write."

"It's Thanksgiving already?"

"Almost."

"Wow, that came fast."

"Not fast enough for me. It means that Christmas is just around the corner. Do you think we'll get snow this year?"

"I'm still focused on the coming turkey. Your mom invited me to join you for dinner."

"Well, of course. You're like one of the family, you know. Where did you have Thanksgiving dinner last year?"

"At the diner near my house. Then I joined some of the guys from work to watch football."

KC leaned over and gave Nick a kiss. "You can have turkey and football with us this year, and every year from now on. Okay?"

Nick smiled shyly. "Okay."

***

"These past few weeks have just flown by. I can hardly wait to see the turkey and pumpkin pie that your mother promised."

"Well, they may have flown by for you, but they have been moving at a snail's pace for me. I have looked at every website online created for those adopted kids and birth parents and siblings looking for each other. I followed even the slightest lead, spent hours at the library, and I am back to square one. No daughter."

"What are you going to do now?"

"I'm considering approaching Caroline anyway. What if she has already found her daughter, and we have invested this much time and effort for nothing?"

"That's a possibility. Hang in there, KC. You still have a few weeks before your deadline."

"Hey, before we get to my parent's house, I should warn you."

"Warn me? About what?"

"Not what, who."

"Geoffrey?"

"No, not Geoffrey. He may be there, of course. Mom never lets anyone eat alone on Thanksgiving. The warning is about my cousins."

"You have cousins?"

"Oh, yes, I have cousins. Three boys. Dad's brother's kids."

"Are they teenagers or something?"

"No, they are younger than I am by just a few years. We spent so much time together as kids that it was like having three brothers. They are all grown up on the outside, but they are still obnoxious little boys on the inside."

"Aw, come on. It can't be that bad."

"You have not met them—yet! Remember, you've been warned."

KC pulled up into the driveway, next to an old station wagon. The front door of the house sported a Christmas wreath in shades of green and blue, with bells hanging from a golden cord announcing their arrival as they went inside.

"Early Christmas is contagious." Nick whispered as they made their way into the kitchen.

"Mom, we're here!" KC announced unnecessarily, as her mother finished drying her hands on a red and green plaid dish towel with reindeer embroidered on it, and gave her a big hug and a kiss on the cheek.

"Yes, Mom, we're here." Nick added, and was rewarded by a generous hug of his own.

"Do you need any help?"

"No, KC, I've got everything under control."

"Are you sure?"

"Everyone is in the living room watching some sports thing on television. Go introduce Nick."

"Are you ready?" KC grabbed Nick's arm and led him into the living room.

"Hello! This is Nick."

"Nick, good to see you again!" KC's father glanced up but stayed in his chair, and reached for some of the chips and dip sitting on the coffee table. "Help yourself."

A man who looked like a slightly younger version of her father stood up and introduced himself, shaking hands. "Nick, I've heard so much about you. Call me Louie, or Uncle Louie if you'd like. My wife, Donna." Donna waved and turned back to the game, and Louie immediately sat back down and grabbed some pretzels. Geoffrey said hello from his perch on the chair next to the window.

The three young men lounging on the carpet in front of the TV set stood up, and began to move toward them.

"Nick, meet John, James, and Jed."

"Well, look who's here! It's Kerry Christmas!"

"Yeah, Kerry Christmas and her boyfriend Nick. Hey, that's good! Saint Nick!"

"KC, come and get a bear hug."

"No way, not again. Come on, guys, take it easy on me this year." KC began to back away.

Her protests went unnoticed, as all three cousins surrounded her and moved in for a big bear hug. Nick would have stepped in to help her, if he had not been so busy laughing.

"Kerry Christmas? The 'C' stands for Christmas?"

"She never told you?"

"Not a word."

John, the tallest of the three, came up to Nick and thumped him on the back. "Yep, born on Christmas Eve."

KC managed to break out of the other's hold, and one warning look from her sent them scurrying back to their places on the floor in front of the TV.

"Let's get some fresh air." Nick led KC through the kitchen, to the bench outside on the patio.

"Kerry Christmas."

"Yes, daughter of Ken and Mary, born on Christmas Eve."

"And you love Christmas? So many people who have a birthday that close to the holidays grow up hating it."

"Yeah, I've heard that. The old 'here is your birthday/Christmas present thing'. But I have always loved Christmas. And my folks worked hard to make Christmas Eve feel like my special day. When I was little, I thought all of those church bells were ringing for me. I felt very special."

"You are very special." Nick leaned toward her and pulled her into his arms for a long kiss.

"Break it up, kids. The turkey is done."

"Thanks, Mom."

"Yeah, thanks, Mom."

Two extra leaves had been put into the table, extending it the entire length of the dining room. A burgundy, brocade table cloth covered the span, and white plates with silver trim were adorned with white napkins folded into silver napkin rings in the shape of little turkeys. In the center a long, low, centerpiece of assorted greenery and red and yellow mums was draped with silver beaded garlands. Orange candles glowed in the middle.

Nick and KC carried the various dishes from the kitchen to the antique sideboard. The huge basket of fresh homemade rolls was set at one end of the table, with one roll disappearing into Nick's mouth on the way in from the kitchen. The other end of the table remained empty until everyone was seated, when KC's dad brought in the huge, beautifully browned turkey and placed it on the table with a dramatic flourish.

"Let's pray before I take a knife to this monster." Everyone held hands, even the unruly cousins.

"Thank you, Lord, for this feast, for friends and family to share it with, and for your Salvation through Christ Jesus, in whose name we pray. Amen."

***

Nick grabbed another roll out of the basket as KC opened a plastic bag to use for the left-overs.

"You cannot possibly have any more room in there!" KC poked him in the stomach.

"No, but these are so good! That was by far the best Thanksgiving dinner I have ever had."

KC's mother walked through the kitchen on her way outside for their customary after-dinner walk. "Hurry up in there, it looks like it might rain. There is plenty of food left for you to snack on later."

The air was cool and refreshing after the huge meal in the crowded room. Louie, Donna and the boys had just left, and Geoffrey had taken an emergency phone call just as dessert was being served, and took a slice of pie to go. Dad, Mom, Nick and KC walked quietly through the neighborhood. Lights were turned on in the windows that they passed, illuminating families, and couples, and friends, joining together at tables.

KC could not help but think of Caroline Smith, eating her Thanksgiving dinner all alone, or with business acquaintances. And what of her daughter? Was she alone, or surrounded by family and friends?

I will find you, and neither of you will spend another Thanksgiving without the other.

They made it back from their walk just as the skies opened up and the sound of the rain blotted out all other noise.

"Mom and I are going to watch *Miracle on 34th Street*. KC, would you like to make up the tray?"

"Sure. Nick and I will take care of it."

"Tray?"

"Yes, it's our tradition. Can you grab the big, silver tray from the sideboard?"

In the kitchen, KC pulled out all of the leftovers that they had worked to put away just hours before. With a practiced hand, she carved enough turkey for four sandwiches, added a little bit of this and that, and set four pieces of pumpkin pie on saucers, complete with whipped cream. Nick made some hot decaf tea and carried the mugs on a smaller tray, while KC delivered the larger one to the coffee table.

"This is great! I have never seen this movie before."

"You mean the old version?"

"No, I mean the movie."

"You poor, deprived guy. There are multiple newer versions, but the original from 1947 still holds the place of honor at our house."

They sat around and watched the old movie, laughing, making comments, anticipating the dialogue, and eating leftovers. Nick made himself comfortable on the floor, leaning back against the couch where KC sat covered in her favorite throw. Her parents sat side-by-side on the other end of the couch, holding hands.

When the movie was over, Dad asked, "Well, Nick, do you have the Christmas spirit now?"

"Is this a trick question?"

"You catch on fast. You had better get your rest tonight, because first thing tomorrow morning, Christmas begins."

***

THE STORY OF THE YEAR

'Christmas begins' was the understatement of the century. By the time Nick woke up the following morning, Christmas had erupted all over the house. A giant garland adorned the mantle. The fall landscape painting that had hung above the fireplace the night before had been replaced with a cool snow scene. Boxes sat on every chair and covered the coffee table, as KC and her mother unwrapped Santas and snowmen and angels, and set them on the bookshelves and side tables.

"Nick, good morning. Have you had breakfast?"

"Not yet, I just got up."

"Well, help yourself." With that, KC turned back to the task at hand, removing the large figures from a ceramic Nativity set to place carefully on the desk next to the window.

Nick ventured toward the kitchen, passing the dining room where the sideboard was now covered with a tiny Christmas village, complete with houses and churches and stores, lights shining from the windows. In the kitchen, he poured himself a cup of coffee and grabbed one of the sweet rolls that had magically appeared overnight.

"Get your jacket. We men have light detail."

Nick followed KC's father outside, to find the front porch covered with boxes marked 'Christmas Lights' stacked three high.

"How many lights do you put up?"

"Always a few strings more than the previous year, Son. Gotta keep up with the neighbors!"

THIRTY-FOUR

The turkey soup that KC had brought back from her parent's house was simmering on her little stove when Nick arrived. She had tucked away a few of the rolls, out of Nick's reach, and now set them out on the table along with her mismatched bowls and glasses of water.

"Ah, another feast. I'm not sure I have any more room."

"Yeah, I know what you mean. But I think we will manage."

Dinner was finished off at a leisurely pace, as they discussed the news of the day, the weather, anything to avoid talking about the story.

"Let's get these dishes washed and get to work, KC. Something must have turned up by now that will help."

"I've been telling myself that all day, as I finished decorating my apartment for Christmas. I did not even turn on my tablet to check my email."

"I noticed the decorations. The right corner of your desk has about six inches without a knickknack on it."

"Very funny. I'll have you know that I have had some of these Christmas decorations since I was a kid."

"Like that funny reindeer with only three feet hanging on the front door?"

"It has sentimental value."

"Uh huh."

"Shall we get to work?"

"Yes."

KC sat down on the couch next to Nick and opened her tablet. As was typical, her social media pages were full of Thanksgiving greetings and Christmas ads after the long weekend.

"Here's one."

"I am not the young mother you were looking for, but I work for an attorney who helps adopted children find their birth parents, especially for medical reasons. Knowing your medical history can be so important. Here is a website devoted specifically to that function. Good luck, and I look forward to reading your next column."

"Well, it may just be the lead we were looking to find."

"I'm on it!"

KC and Nick spent the next several hours researching, starting with the web link that the reader had provided. When there was nothing on that site that matched the criteria they were looking for, they tried other similar sites. They found nothing that could help them.

"I'm sorry, KC. I have been praying for you and for Caroline and her daughter. Surrounded by Christmas like this, I still believe you can make this reunion happen. I have faith in you. It's the season for miracles, right?"

"I have been praying, too. But I have to admit, I'm tired. Partly because it is late, of course, but also just tired of all of the dead ends."

What if I have to reveal Caroline's identity to salvage this story? What will Nick think of me then?

It was close to eleven when KC gave up on the websites and turned off her computer. The little ding from her tablet that announced a new email made her jump, and she stopped herself in motion, and opened her email app.

***

"I have just now caught up on reading the newspaper for the past few months. I have been away from home, dealing with a family medical crisis, but I love your column and did not want to miss anything. I found out that I was adopted many years ago, but never gave much thought to my birth parents. While I waited at the hospital each day, the thought of finding out about my roots had crossed my mind. My grandson has been very ill, and they tell me there may be a genetic connection. Imagine my surprise, when I go home and read the information in your columns about the little red diary. I was born on Dec 24, 1954 at 5:47 p.m. at Mercy General

Hospital in Sacramento. My mother—my adoptive mother, said I was a tiny thing, only five pounds and ten ounces according to my birth certificate. I have red hair and green eyes, although I was told they were blue when I was first born. If this information is in line with your research, please feel free to call me at . . . I live in Hillsboro, just outside of Portland.

 Sandra Wentworth"

***

"This is it! We've found Caroline's daughter!"

"Slow down a bit, KC. This looks really, really promising. But remember Doris Smith. Let's get a good night's sleep and you can contact Sandra Wentworth in the morning and make arrangements to meet with her. Maybe tomorrow if that works with her schedule. I'll go with you if you would like."

"I would like."

"Kiss goodnight?"

His kiss and the late hour left her unusually speechless. She was in her pajamas and tucked into bed just minutes after Nick left. She fell asleep quickly with a smile on her face.

***

"What time is it?"

"KC, you asked me just a few minutes ago. It is not quite noon. She'll be here."

The door to the little sandwich shop opened as if on cue, and a woman entered. She looked around and came right over to the table where KC and Nick were sitting.

"KC Adams? I recognize you both from your pictures in the paper."

KC stood up and extended her hand, looking down into the smiling face of the petite woman. Her hair was still mostly red, with gray streaks on the sides adding an air of distinction.

"You must be Sandra. You have no idea how happy I am to meet you."

"How nice! I was rather excited to get your call. Do you think I might be the daughter of the woman who wrote the diary?"

"I think it is a distinct possibility. Did you bring your birth certificate?"

Sandra produced an official copy of the birth certificate, along with some photos of herself as a baby, a young child, a teenager, and an adult. The resemblance to Caroline Smith was striking, but KC kept her thoughts to herself.

"This is a photo of myself and my family from last Christmas. Henry, the baby, is the little guy who has been so sick."

"The baby is named Henry?"

"Yes. It was my son-in-law's grandfather's name."

Nick spoke up. "Sandra, it is a real pleasure to meet you. There is no doubt that this birth certificate is real, and that you are who you say you are. You mentioned to KC over the phone that you are a widow?"

"Yes, my husband died several years ago in a car accident. He would have been so thrilled to be a part of this."

"I'm so sorry for your loss."

KC was busy looking at the photo of the family, with a younger version of Sandra holding a baby, both with red hair. "Is this your daughter?"

"Yes, that's my Sara. Here she is in a photo from last Christmas. And the tall, handsome, dark-haired guy in the background is my son, Timothy, with my daughter-in-law, Sadie. Their twin girls, Jean and Jane, are ten this year. Sara's husband, Mike, was the one taking the picture, so he's the only one not in the photo. Their three children are Mike Jr., now twelve, Cindy, who is five, and the baby, Henry, who will be two this January. And of course, there I am in the middle, with that silly grin on my face that I get whenever I am with them. I wrote all of the names on the back of the photo for you."

"May I keep these photos for a while?"

"Oh course, I have extra copies."

"Sandra, I have no doubt that you are the daughter we have been searching for, the baby from the diary."

"Really? That is wonderful! What happens next?"

What does happen next?

Nick spoke up. "Next, KC and I go to Sacramento. Right, KC?"

"Yes. We will schedule a meeting with the woman who wrote the diary and tell her about finding the book and our search for her daughter, and arrange the reunion with the two of you."

"You mean she doesn't know?"

KC spoke up. "No, she doesn't. I did not want to get her hopes up if we could not find you."

"What if she does not want to meet me?"

What if she does not want to meet her?

"Sandra, KC is one of the most persuasive women I know." Nick patted her on the shoulder. "Have a little faith."

"Oh, I have a lot of faith. In the Lord who loves me and forgave my sins. In a family that God has brought through some perilous times these past few months. And I have faith in you, KC."

"Thank you, Sandra. I won't let you down."

***

"I'm glad you decided to take your truck. I usually love the snow, but I hate driving in it, especially on the freeway. Thank you."

"You're welcome."

"It was beautiful going through the passes, though, wasn't it?"

"My eyes were on the road and the crazy people that went speeding past me as if it was not snowing hard. This truck has four-wheel-drive, but it is not license to be stupid on the road."

"Yes, it did get a little dicey back there, but so lovely. When we passed Dunsmuir, it looked like a perfect little postcard town, covered in snow, tucked away against the mountains."

"You enjoy the view, I'll drive. We'll stop for dinner once we get to a little lower elevation."

"Sounds good. I'm sorry we got such a late start, but Mr. Knitzer wanted to meet with me before I left."

"You never did tell me what he said."

"He said, in a nutshell, if I don't get the woman who wrote the diary to agree to the reunion, then I had better be prepared to print a story about her anyway. Either way, he has decided that he wants me to include her name."

"Or what?"

"Or I'm out of a job."

"Oh, brother! Where are his ethics?"

"He just wants the story. He's a newspaper man, and that is the bottom line for him. He does not care about hurting people's feelings, or interrupting their privacy."

"What do you plan to do?"

What am I going to do? I don't want to think about it right now.

"I'm going to take it one day at a time. The snow has let up, and there is a good place to eat just a few miles down the freeway. How about stopping there?"

Nick agreed, and the matter was closed for the moment.

They arrived at the hotel in Sacramento later that evening, trapped in rush hour traffic an hour longer than they had planned.

The next morning dawned wet and cloudy. KC met Nick in the hotel coffee shop, and they ate their breakfast quietly.

"When is our meeting with Caroline Smith?"

"Not until 11:30. She agreed to meet at her office."

"Did you tell her why we were meeting with her?"

"Not exactly."

"What do you mean by that?"

"I told her I was a reporter and wanted an interview."

Nick's loud sigh said enough. KC knew that she should have been more open with Caroline about the reason for the meeting.

"I know, I know. But, really, do you think she would have agreed to see me if I had shared my real purpose?"

"We'll never know, will we? KC, have you prayed about this meeting?"

Silence.

"Would you like to pray together now?"

"Yes."

"Lord, please prepare Caroline's heart, let it be open, and let her be willing to accept her daughter back into her life. Whatever happens, we leave the situation in Your hands. Amen."

"Thank you. I am so used to just barreling through situations on my own, I forget that God is there beside me."

"He is always there, KC. I'm here, too."

"I know."

"Meet you in the lobby at 10:30? We don't have to go far, but I don't know how much traffic we will encounter."

***

The building that housed Smith and Johnson, Inc., was large and impressive from the outside. Tall windows reflected back the cloudy skies, as KC and Nick made their way from the parking garage to the front entrance. KC did not know what to expect, but from her first encounter with Carol Smith at the garden presentation, she thought the lobby would be cool and impersonal. It was just the opposite. Warm, cocoa brown walls were lined with photographs from the early days of the Smith family history. Frontiersmen, gold miners, businessmen, all showed the progression of wealth this family had earned. The senator's photo, larger than the rest and framed in dark mahogany, was in the center of the photo gallery. Carol Smith's picture was surprisingly small and placed inconspicuously at the end of the wall. It had obviously been taken when she was much younger, perhaps after her father had died and she took over the business. Even at that young age, her eyes held a seriousness that was perceptible, even in a two-dimensional photograph. Still, KC could see Sandra's resemblance to Caroline in those serious green eyes.

"Ms. Adams? Ms. Smith will see you now."

Nick and KC followed the impeccably dressed young woman to the office at the end of the hall. The corner of the building allowed for wide views of the city from the east and the south. A large but simple desk sat at a diagonal between the windows. At that angle, the person sitting there would have their back to the city. How peculiar.

"KC Adams?" Carol Smith rose from the desk and reached to shake KC's hand.

"My associate, Nick Evans."

"Hmm. Your associate. I read your column about the fire this past summer, Ms. Adams, and I believe that this is your firefighter hero? Please, sit down, both of you. How may I help you?"

She certainly gets right to the point.

"So you have not read my column recently?"

"No, I have not. I am an extremely busy woman. I am curious, though, as to why a newspaper reporter from Oregon would want an interview with me."

"Ms. Smith, does this look familiar?" KC produced the red diary from her backpack.

Caroline Smith gave an almost imperceptible gasp, but her stoic expression never wavered. "What does this book have to do with me?"

"I found this accidentally when I was the fire watcher at Iliana Lookout. It was hidden under the bed. Nick had taken it out of the lookout before the fire, and so it was safe. I have been writing a series of articles based on the information found in this diary."

"Again, I ask, what does this have to do with me?"

"The diary was written by a young woman in 1955, a woman who had lost her true love, and had given up her newborn daughter for adoption. I determined to find the mother and her child and reunite them. By Christmas."

"What nonsense! Who would care about something that happened so many years ago?"

"Apparently, a lot of people. My columns have generated more readers than the newspaper has seen in a long time. Those readers are waiting to hear what happens when the two women are reunited."

"What does all of this have to do with me? I am a very busy woman, and I do not have time for riddles. Get to the point."

"Caroline, I believe that you are the young mother who wrote the diary."

"Nonsense. I have no children; I have never been married. If your research has led you to me, then you have made a mistake. I am not that woman. I did not write that diary."

I didn't see this coming. What do I do now, Lord?

"Caroline . . ."

"It is Carol. No one has called me Caroline in many, many years. You may call me Ms. Smith."

"Ms. Smith, I tracked down Kathryn's daughter, Beth, who remembers meeting Dottie when she was very young. Her mother's friend had just come from the Iliana Fire Lookout. I was able to find you in the Sacramento High School yearbook, and Dottie was your nickname."

"I am not the person you are seeking. I am sorry that you came all this way for nothing." Caroline rose and gestured toward the door. "I have a lunch meeting to attend."

"Caroline—Ms. Smith, at least look at these photos of your daughter and her family." KC tossed the prints down onto the desk, spreading them out so that the faces were clearly visible.

Caroline did not even glance down at them. "I'm sorry, Ms. Adams, this meeting is over. If you try to use my name to sell your newspapers, you will be hearing from my attorney."

KC laid a card with Sandra's name and address on the desk next to the photographs. "This is the contact information for your daughter, Sandra. I will be meeting with her at her home at noon on December 18th and give her the diary at that time. She should at least know that she was loved when she was born, even if she is not now."

With that final word, KC walked out of the office with her head held high, and a tear sliding down her cheek. Nick followed closely behind.

THIRTY-FIVE

"You are not seriously considering revealing Caroline Smith's identity?"

"Why not? After that awful interview with her, I think my attempts to protect her privacy are wasted. Have you ever met such a cold fish? I am so angry with her rejection of Sandra and refusal to even look at the photographs that we drove over ten hours to bring to her."

"KC, I know you are furious with Caroline. It is understandable. You have put months of research and hard work into this story, expecting a wonderful and touching outcome. You have to accept the facts."

"The facts are that Caroline was right. The woman who wrote the diary and the woman who sat behind that desk are not the same person."

"Who knows what changed her. Perhaps the years of focusing only on her work has hardened her heart."

"I don't think she has a heart."

"I wonder if she has any faith in God remaining."

"I think she has faith in the dollar and her own power. Imagine threatening me with a lawsuit if I print her name? I should do it just because of that. She can't fight freedom of the press!"

"I understand that you are angry KC, but please promise me that you will not write your next column until you take the time to pray about it and calm down first."

"Yeah, yeah."

"Yes? You will not write your column while you are still angry?"

"I'm going to go for a walk and think it over."

"Okay. That's probably a good idea. I wish I was there to give you a big hug and let you know that you are not alone in this."

"Thanks, Nick. I know you care. I just have to work this one out on my own."

"I know you will do the right thing and keep Caroline's name a secret."

"Don't push it, Nick."

"I love you."

"I love you, too."

KC pulled on her boots and threw her raincoat on over her sweatshirt and yoga pants, then shoved a knitted hat over her tousled hair, not bothering to take her umbrella. She needed to walk off her anger and let her professional training and instincts take over. She needed to let go of the anger and pray about this situation.

The rain-soaked sidewalks splashed water up past her boots and onto the hem of her long raincoat, which then dripped back down into the tops of her boots. She did not notice, as she walked briskly along, block after block disappearing behind her as she weighed her options and wrote and rewrote her next column in her head.

Revealing Caroline Smith as the young mother from the diary would have huge consequences. Her column would likely be picked up by the mainstream press and go viral on the Internet. It could well be the story of the year. She would gain national attention overnight. Mr. Knitzer would be thrilled, and she would keep her job. Caroline deserved it, after her response to her meeting with KC. But did Sandra deserve to have her story revealed in such a public and harsh way? And what about Nick? If KC went against what he so clearly felt was right, would it permanently damage their relationship? What would God want her to do?

I know, Lord, I know. I guess I've known all along.

A car honked as KC was about to cross the street, and then turned right in front of her, the tires splashing water from the curb right up over the sidewalk and filling her boots with the cold, muddy runoff from the street. KC broke out laughing, then sloshed her way back home to change her wet clothes and write her column.

***

On the Lookout with KC Adams

December 13

The mystery of the red diary is nearly solved! I want to thank all of my readers who have sent me emails, messages and comments on my social media pages, and countless letters. Together we have pieced together the clues left to us in an old book hidden beneath the bed in the Iliana Lookout Tower since 1955.

I often wonder what would have happened if the circumstances had been different. What if the bat had not flown into the tower? What if I had not been brave enough to challenge that bat, and break the bed in the process? What if I had never noticed the old, dusty diary lying on the floor beneath the bed? Of course, the most dramatic circumstance was the fire that sent me running down the mountain, as it destroyed the Iliana Lookout Tower and everything else in its wake. I ask myself, what if Nick had not taken the diary with him a few days earlier?

Yet here it is, the red diary, held in my hands for one last time. It has led us all on quite an adventure. For those readers who are just catching up, here is a review.

A young woman had lost her true love when he died suddenly. She was left carrying his daughter, and out of love for the child, gave her up for adoption. Together we determined that the diary was written in 1955. From the description of a memorable fire and a comment in the diary that the baby would be six months old the following day, we determined that the birthdate was December 24, 1954. Pages from the diary that described a place called Capitol Park and referenced Thirteenth Street, along with a mention of a purple dragon, led us to conclude that the young woman came from Sacramento, California.

THE STORY OF THE YEAR

I shared with you my excitement when I found the identity of the woman who wrote the diary, and traveled to Sacramento to find out if my research was correct. I will not comment on that right now. This week's column will be devoted to someone very special.

I have found the daughter!

Your feedback and suggestions gave me so many good leads, but in the end, our mystery was solved through a simple email from a woman who lived in a town just outside of Portland.

Her name is Sandra. She is a woman who is beautiful inside and out. There was a description of the baby in the diary, describing her as looking just like her father, and Sandra matches that description completely. She bears a very strong resemblance to the mother as well. She was born on December 24, 1954, at Mercy General Hospital in Sacramento, and was adopted and raised in a very loving home.

So, who is this woman, this daughter, the baby so loved by the young woman who wrote the diary? Sandra is a widow, the mother of a son and a daughter, and grandmother to five sweet boys and girls. When we met for the first time, I felt an automatic connection to her. She could easily be your friend, your aunt, your teacher. In fact, Sandra taught school for many years, and has just recently retired. She is a woman of faith, and gives much of her time to helping her church, including a local shelter for unwed mothers.

The email that I received from Sandra came quite late in my search, because she has been out of town, helping her daughter care for her youngest grandchild, who suffers from a serious illness. I am happy to report that he is doing better, but the expenses for the family have been extremely high. This paper has set up an Internet fund account. If you wish to donate, please go to the paper's main web page and click on the link 'Henry'. You will be able to read the specifics there.

My interview with Sandra led to one important piece of information that she asked me to share with you. The doctors believe that there may be a genetic predisposition to the illness that has caused so much suffering for her grandson. Sandra had been considering looking for her birth parents to find out the medical history for her family, when she read my column, and the truth of her birth unfolded. She would like those of you who have been adopted or have given a child up for adoption, to consider making a connection for the purpose of exchanging this information, whether or not you are looking for a relationship with them.

Now I know what you are all thinking. Christmas is just around the corner. Will there be a reunion between the mother and child? Read my column on December 20th and find out.

Until next week,

KC Adams

***

KC received good feedback from her readers on her column about Sandra. Money came pouring in to the fund set up in her grandson's name. The comments from Sandra regarding the possible genetic link to the illness and the discussion on knowing your family medical history made a strong impression. People who had responded earlier that they did not want any contact with their birth parents, wrote her that they were reconsidering.

As she sent the column in to the paper, KC wondered briefly if Caroline Smith would read it. Somehow, after the disastrous meeting in Sacramento, she doubted it.

It had snowed for several days, and although KC loved it, especially around Christmas, her heart was just not into the festivities this year. Her reputation as a writer and her job at the newspaper were sitting precariously on the edge, ready to fall at any moment. She sat quietly at her office Christmas party, though Nick managed to keep the conversations going with her workmates. Mr. Knitzer had not backed down on his insistence that she reveal the name of the mother.

What am I supposed to do, Lord?

***

It was December 18th, and Nick was due to arrive in just a few minutes to drive her to Hillsboro to meet with Sandra. The red diary was tucked into her backpack for the last time. She was almost sad at the thought of giving it away, it had been such a part of her life for so long. Yet, Sandra deserved to know something about the father that had died before she was born, and the mother that had loved her enough to want a real family for her. Perhaps giving Sandra the diary would be some compensation for not having the reunion with her mother that she had been promised. KC had not spoken with Sandra about the circumstances yet, deciding to tell her about it face-to-face.

The car horn honked from outside, a signal that Nick had kept the motor and the heater running.

"You look very Christmassy today!" Nick leaned over and gave KC a kiss on the cheek.

She looked down at her red wool coat with the sparkling holly pin on the lapel, and the dark green turtleneck peeking up over the collar. "I tried."

"Are you okay?"

"Yes, I'm fine. I have been praying nonstop all morning, and I have a strange peace that whatever happens today, everything will be as it is supposed to be."

"That's a great attitude. KC, are you going to tell Sandra the identity of her mother?"

"You know, I keep going back and forth about that. Does she deserve to know? Yes, especially with her questions about the medical history."

"What if Caroline denies it, or worse yet, refuses to have any contact with her?"

"I've thought of that too. That would be a crushing blow to me, if I were in Sandra's place."

"Perhaps. I think you are actually closer to this than Sandra, after all of your work. Make sure the feelings that you are concerned about are not your own."

"You are right. I can't seem to completely get over my anger and frustration. I could tell Sandra everything, print Caroline's name, keep my job, and the sensationalism could make this the story of the year. I've also asked myself if Caroline deserves to keep her secret, after refusing to accept her daughter."

"What would God want you to do?"

"I've been praying about that all morning."

"And?"

"And I have decided that the answer is yes, Caroline deserves her privacy, despite her cold attitude toward her daughter. Whether I like it or not, whether I think it is the right thing for her to do, in the end, it is not up to me."

"You are not going to tell Sandra about Caroline."

"No, I'm not. I am going to give her the dairy, so that she can know that she was loved."

"If you give her the dairy, she may figure out the mystery herself."

"Perhaps, but it is not likely. She does not have our skills and resources."

"I love you."

"Despite my temptations and anger?"

"You are not giving in to those, are you? That is one of the things I love about you. You do know that my love for you would not have changed even if you had decided to tell the world about Caroline?"

"Really?"

"Really."

"Oh, this is our exit!"

"Got it. Thanks."

Nick pulled up in the driveway of a gray ranch style house. White shutters and railings on the porch added a nice touch, as did the topiaries in pots that flanked the front door, which was painted a darker gray. A Christmas wreath in festive red and green hung on the front door, which opened as they walked up on the porch.

"KC, Nick, how nice to see you again! Would you like to come in? We will have to be quiet, little Henry is asleep on the couch."

"That's okay, Sandra, we can talk right here. I have something to give you."

KC reached into her backpack and pulled out the old, red diary.

"Oh, my goodness, is that for me?" Sandra took it gently.

"I want you to know that your mother loved your father, and she loved you. As you read these pages, keep in mind how young she was at the time."

"I understand. In this day and age, it is nothing to have a child out of wedlock. When I was born, that was not the case. I don't fault her for giving me up for adoption. I had a wonderful family and a good life."

"Sandra, I'm sorry to have to tell you this, but . . ."

Just as KC was about to explain to Sandra that her mother did not want a relationship with her, a limousine drove up to the front of the house. Sandra, KC and Nick all turned to look at the car, as the driver came around and opened the door. Caroline Smith, dressed in white from her shoes to her beautiful coat, got out and came toward them on the porch. She gave KC a quick smile as she passed by, but her eyes were on Sandra.

"Sandra? You look so much like your father! I am your mother, Caroline Smith. You may call me Dottie."

As the two women hugged, KC and Nick quietly backed off of the porch and headed for their truck. This reunion deserved to be kept private.

***

"I can't stop smiling," KC said as they headed back toward the freeway.

"I noticed."

"Isn't this absolutely wonderful?"

"Yep. Absolutely wonderful." Nick reached over and squeezed her hand.

"What a great end to this story, and a marvelous Christmas gift for both women."

"And for you too!"

"Yes, me too. Hey, you missed the on-ramp."

"I'm taking a shortcut home."

They drove east through quiet roads, past homes decked out with Christmas lights, and dark barns that stood out against the gray sky.

"Where are we going?"

"We're almost there. Be patient."

Forest Park was the unexpected destination. Nestled along the banks of the Willamette River, where blue water cascaded over mossy boulders, they walked along a little trail. No one else had ventured out on this wet, cold afternoon. Nick reached out and held KC's hand, and they walked silently as a few light snowflakes began to fall.

"This is magic."

"Being with you is magic."

THE STORY OF THE YEAR

Nick led KC up onto a little bridge where the water trickled below and the snow fell above. He let go of her hand briefly, as he reached into his jacket pocket for a little red box.

"Oh!" KC gasped.

Nick dropped to one knee. "Kerry Christmas Adams, will you marry me?"

"Yes! Oh, yes!"

He stood and slid the diamond ring onto her left hand, then held her in his arms, and their kiss sealed the promise.

***

KC smiled as she folded the newspaper and placed it carefully on her father's desk. She had waited up until the early hours of the morning to collect the paper from the front porch the moment it had been delivered. Nick came from behind and placed his arm warmly around her shoulders. She reached up and linked her hand with his, her engagement ring sparkling as it caught the light from the lamp.

"Is it too early to say Merry Christmas? Just five more days!"

KC smiled up at him. "I had a brief email from Mr. Knitzer. He loved my column. He said that he has an idea for . . ."

Nick interrupted her with a kiss. "We will take on your next adventure after the first of the year, if that's OK with you."

"Mmm. Perfect."

"Will you read it to me, KC?"

He picked up the paper and led her to the little loveseat in the office. The rest of the house was dark and quiet as she opened the paper and began to read.

***

On the Lookout with KC Adams

December 20

I have taken you with me on this amazing journey through the past. From the words written in an old, red diary, found in a fire lookout tower on the top of a mountain, we waded through the mysteries and clues together. As I struggled through dead ends and promising leads, your best wishes and advice poured in. You stayed with me every step of the way as I worked to reunite a mother and daughter.

This intriguing story has been a lot like the mystery of Christmas itself.

That first Christmas, when God sent His Son to earth as a tiny baby. Knowing that His ultimate sacrifice for us would be the greatest gift of all. How can we ever comprehend such love?

Perhaps life is like the mysteries of this Christmas, as you and your children await the surprises hidden under the wrapping paper, bows, and ribbons concealing the secrets inside.

I did find a daughter, one who was not yet searching for the mother who gave her life, the mother who was courageous enough to give her away to a loving family. A daughter with children and grandchildren of her own, who has learned the value of sacrificial love. A woman who has struggled with life's trials and problems, and through her courage and unwavering faith, has never ceased to show unconditional love to her family.

I also found the mother, the heartsick woman who wrote that impassioned journal, crying out for the man she had lost and for the child she had let go out of love.

You want to know the name of the woman who wrote the diary. You want to see a picture of the meeting of mother and daughter, to witness the dramatic embrace. Does this Christmas story have the happy ending we have all come to expect from the books and movies?

Let me ask you this first.

THE STORY OF THE YEAR

How many children are out there tonight, estranged from their parents? How many parents, crying for their children? How many sisters, brothers, or friends with broken relationships? Christmas is a time of great joy, but also a time of great sadness for so many. When the separation is death, the chasm is too great to cross. Yet, if you are separated from your loved one because of anger or misunderstanding, differing opinions, harsh words spoken that you think cannot be taken back, it is not too late for you.

You can be courageous too, this Christmas. You can make that phone call, that visit. You can send that email or that letter. You can offer the first hug, the first 'I'm sorry', the first 'I love you'. What if the surprise under the tree this year is a renewal of hope, a reconnection with someone lost, or the reuniting of family?

Yesterday, I delivered the diary to a daughter, who now knows without a doubt how much she was loved. In the words in that little red book from so many years ago, a mother's heart cried out for her child. Yesterday, the mother and child were reunited in a scene both touching and tender. The names and place do not matter. The love that spanned those years apart came to life before my eyes. Such was the miracle I was honored to witness this Christmas season.

In a few days, I will celebrate with my own family. And I will share Christmas this year with the hero who saved me not only from a fire, but from my own fears and lack of faith, and now offers me a lifetime of love.

Love . . . that is my wish for each of you.

Merry Christmas,

KC Adams

About the Author

BONNIE HOWELL lives on the beautiful North Umpqua River in Oregon with her husband, Joe, their dog, Shadow, and the computer, Lucifer. A lifelong storyteller, she writes poetry, children's tales, and books of romance and faith. Her greatest joy is to share stories of God's love for us, and of the journey of a man and a woman to love each other.

And now these three remain: faith, hope and love.
But the greatest of these is love.

I Corinthians 13:13

Made in the USA
San Bernardino, CA
05 April 2017